She'd almost d... a virgin!

She met his gaze and willingly let it take hold of her. There was no question in her mind what his thoughts were, or what his husky tone implied. His eyes said it all—that he desired her, that he'd be wonderful to her if she would stay with him tonight.

Terra found herself thinking, Yes, yes, yes. Her gaze dropped to the firm, sensual shape of his lips and prompted a relentless urge to kiss him, touch him, put her whole self in his hands. The man was perfect. So perfect that she wasn't tense. The mood was ideal and for the first time in her life she wanted to be swept away.

If she didn't respond to him, and the plane crashed tomorrow, she'd die—as she'd almost died tonight—without ever experiencing a man like this.

STRANGER IN THE NIGHT

BY

ROSEANNE WILLIAMS

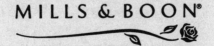

MILLS & BOON®

*All the characters in this book have no existence outside the imagination
of the author, and have no relation whatsoever to anyone bearing the same
name or names. They are not even distantly inspired by any individual
known or unknown to the author, and all the incidents are pure invention.*

*First published in Great Britain 1997
by Harlequin Mills & Boon Limited,
Eton House, 18-24 Paradise Road, Richmond, Surrey TW9 1SR*

© Harlequin Books S.A. 1996
Roseanne Williams is acknowledged as the author of this work.

ISBN 0 263 80511 5

21-9708

Printed and bound in Great Britain

Roseanne Williams is also the author of these novels in *Temptation*®:

THE MAGIC TOUCH
LOVE CONQUERS ALL
UNDER THE COVERS
THE BAD BOY
SEEING RED
MAIL ORDER MAN
A TRUE BLUE KNIGHT
SECOND-HAND BRIDE

Prologue

"SO, ARE WE GOING to the boat party, the pool party and the beach party tonight?" Jilly asked.

"None of the above," Terra Camden muttered from where she was flopped on the bed in the Myrtle Beach motel room she had shared with her friends, Jilly and Fallon, for three days.

Tomorrow, they'd fly home from South Carolina, and she would be glad to return to San Francisco where she and her roommates were college students. Spring break had sounded like great fun at the start, but Terra had found it more exhausting than exciting.

Watching her two exhilarated roommates prepare for a fourth night of spring revelry made her all the more homesick. She even missed her natural hair color, having bleached it from brown to surfer blond for the occasion.

"Party pooper," Fallon taunted with a puckish smile, while she put on mascara. "As if you've OD'd on having a wild and crazy time."

"Not," Jilly drawled, polishing her toenails.

Terra pretended to snore. "Marathon beer parties and recreational sex aren't my things, it turns out. Yours, yes, but not mine."

Fallon rolled her eyes. "They're what spring break is all about—letting loose, pulling out all the stops."

"I know, I know, but—"

"No buts," Jilly countered. "This is our last night, for heaven's sake. Get up, get with it and give it your best."

Fallon chimed in, "Think of the thousands of stud muffins out there, hard up and willing to be yours tonight. Take your pick."

"I just want to go home." Terra groaned, painfully aware that she was the only virgin in the room. Jilly and Fallon were vastly experienced and never minced words about it.

For sure, the condoms they'd brought hadn't gone unused, whereas the package in Terra's beach bag still had an unbroken seal. So far, virginity still hounded her, and not even spring break had changed it.

"Get up." Jilly prodded. "Get your act together. Get a move on."

To put them off her case, Terra dragged along to the three parties they'd gotten invited to. First, the beach party, where Jilly and Fallon paired up with two guys. Terra stayed busy sipping one beer and fending off amorous advances from several young men. From there, she went with her friends and their friends to a pool party at someone's house, and finally to a raucous boat party in Charleston Harbor.

It was a split-level houseboat, with music and dancing, and a chug-a-lug contest was in full swing when they arrived. Terra was relieved to be asked to dance by a Duke University senior who seemed nice enough. He stuck around after that, flirting and making small talk.

She didn't mind, since Greg was polite, amusing and his attention kept other guys at bay.

Jilly passed by, slightly tipsy, and drew her aside. "Terra, he's perfect. Cute, great build, all the right stuff for a fling to remember."

"No, I don't think so. I mean, granted he's good-looking, but having a fling with him isn't on my agenda."

"Terra, if you don't lighten up you're going to be a virgin forever. You know?"

"The time just isn't right," Terra replied. "And the mood is definitely wrong."

"Think sexy thoughts, then. Fantasize to the max. It's all in your head, anyway."

"Jilly, no offense but you live your life and I'll live mine, okay?"

"Sure, but in my humble opinion you're missing the time of your life with this guy." Jilly gave Greg an appraising glance, smiled knowingly and sauntered away.

Greg stepped in again. "What was that all about?"

"Nothing much." Terra's head started pounding to the bass beat of the blaring music and the repetitive chants accompanying the beer-drinking contest. "I need some fresh air."

"Follow me," he said.

He took her hand and guided her through a sliding-glass door to an open deck. The door slid closed, shutting in the party and leaving them alone. Terra went to the railing and drew in a deep gulp of air.

"Too much to drink?" Greg asked.

"Probably." She was reluctant to let on how uncool she was. Practically a teetotaler. Positively a virgin.

Homesick, too, not to mention jet lagged. Even her own friends were shaking their heads about her.

Greg smiled and tipped up her chin. "You know what you need?"

"What?"

"Some Southern comfort."

Terra saw that he wanted to kiss her, and she didn't discourage it. Instead, she hoped that it would be enjoyable, possibly exciting. Besides, she wasn't so inexperienced that she didn't know how to make out within her own limits. And this might be the only pleasant memory she'd take home with her.

Greg's lips settled on hers, a bit too greedily perhaps, though not enough to make her recoil with distaste. Not at first. But before very long, his arms were locked around her in an iron grip, pinning her elbows to her sides, and then his tongue snaked into her mouth. Backed up against the deck rail by his hard, insistent body, Terra was dismayed to find herself imprisoned by his strength and silenced by his voracious mouth.

She struggled to break out of his control, to tear her mouth free and yell for him to stop. Or yell for help. But who would hear her above the pounding music? Panic set in as he cut short the coarse, crude kiss and covered her mouth with his hand.

"C'mon, blondie," he panted, grinding his pelvis against her. "Cooperate."

Gagged by his palm, she could only make muffled sounds of fright and outrage. Her desperate efforts to kick his shins were hampered by the rail behind her.

He grunted. "Like it rough, do you?"

She bared her teeth and sank them into his sweaty palm.

"Damn!" His face contorted with pain, he jerked his hand away.

Terra screamed, even though she knew she couldn't be heard inside. She squirmed and kicked, worked one hand free and clawed at him.

She heard a male voice shout from somewhere across the water, "Hey! Knock it off!"

There was a splash, and at the same time there was Greg snarling at her, "Goddamned hellcat!"

Catching a fistful of her waist-length hair, he yanked her head back and ground against her again.

"No!" she screamed.

Revolted and desperate to escape, Terra brought up one knee hard into his crotch. He let go of her hair to clutch both hands over his fly in pained surprise.

Disoriented, terrorized, trembling with fear, Terra saw only one way to escape him. Without hesitation, she climbed over the rail and jumped off the boat.

It didn't matter that she couldn't swim....

Holding her breath, she sank in deep and then thrashed back up to the surface. She glimpsed the boat before sinking a second time, and saw Greg lean over the rail. Flailing her arms and legs, she broke the surface once more.

"Help," she gasped.

"Help yourself," Greg snarled. He turned and went inside.

Never in her life had Terra imagined she'd die by drowning. But now it seemed inevitable as she went under again.

Suddenly, when it seemed that her lungs would burst, something—some*one*—took hold of her and stopped her descent. She felt herself being buoyed upward and then her head cleared the waterline. She sucked in deep, choking breaths.

"Keep calm," a voice said in her ear—not Greg's voice, but the same male voice she'd heard shouting across the water a few minutes earlier.

"C-can't swim," she gasped.

"I've got you. You're safe." The voice was confident, comforting. The arm curled around her middle was strong, unfailing.

Faceup in the dark, chill water, she felt herself being towed away from the houseboat. It came to her that the splash she'd heard earlier must have been this man diving in. She didn't know him, couldn't see what he looked like. All she could see was the star-spangled night sky as he powered her through the water. Still, she could feel how tall and sleek and strong his body was, for it was aligned against her own body as he swam.

She had to trust him, for he was saving her life and taking her, it seemed, to safety.

"Thank you," she got out through her chattering teeth. They wouldn't stop, nor would her body stop shivering.

"Nothing to it. Relax."

She closed her eyes and tried to do as he said. Tried not to think of how close she had come to drowning, or of how foolish she had been to leave San Francisco. This wouldn't have happened if she hadn't traipsed along with Jilly and Fallon. But then, they weren't at fault. Her life was her own responsibility, and now she owed it to a stranger in the night.

"Here's my boat," he said, slowing to a gradual stop. Supported in his arms, she came upright and saw that he'd brought her to a sizable sailboat anchored a short distance offshore from the marina. Dim interior lights were on, giving out a glow through the cabin windows.

"Your boat," she murmured, thinking she'd never seen a more welcome sight. The light from inside gave her a look at the man's face. It was square-jawed...and handsome, she discovered with a shivery thrill. His hair, brows and lashes were dark, spiked with droplets of seawater.

He smiled, a gleam of white in the night. "All aboard, mermaid."

He boosted her up a short rope ladder to the deck of his sailboat and kept a steadying hand on her as he ascended behind her. Then he scooped her up in his powerful arms and carried her below into the cabin.

With her cheek pillowed against the dark hair on his broad chest, Terra became acutely aware that he wore nothing more than his briefs.

"There," he said, setting her down dripping wet in a maple captain's chair. "Catch your breath."

He opened an overhead bin and brought out towels and blankets. Terra wanted to say she was sorry to be a bother, but she couldn't shiver and speak at the same time.

The water had been so shockingly cold, almost paralyzing. However, the sight of her hero's tall, muscular, nearly nude body started an instant warming trend deep inside her. He seemed unaware that his white underwear was almost transparent from being soaked, or that it molded his virile contours and dimensions like a second skin.

He glanced over, caught her eyes on him and gave her a teasing grin. "You like my lifeguard uniform?"

Terra would normally have been mortified to be caught staring in that way, but his casual, disarming sense of humor surprised her into smiling at herself, along with him.

She even came up with a droll reply. "Outstanding."

"I only wear it to rescue mermaids. You're my first," he said as he knelt in front of her chair and tucked a heavy wool blanket around her. Next, he wrapped a thick towel around her head.

When he finished, Terra looked into his eyes and saw that they were a deep, compelling sea blue. His expression was a mixture of concern, amusement and male interest.

"You're my first lifeguard," she murmured, relieved to get her chattering teeth under control. "I don't know how to thank you."

"You don't have to." He stayed kneeling there, gazing at her. Then he frowned. "Did he hurt you?"

Her nasty experience with Greg came back in a rush. "Nothing serious."

"Your boyfriend?"

"No, we met at the party. I never thought a simple kiss would send the wrong message." She shook her head. "He seemed so nice at first."

"Good thing I heard you scream."

She agreed, "I would have drowned if you hadn't come. I owe you my life, and I don't even know your name."

He hesitated a moment. "I don't know yours, either. But I do know something about you."

"Such as, I can't swim," she said, rolling her eyes in self-mockery.

He smiled. "That, and you're beautiful. Simply beautiful."

Terra caught her breath. She saw absolute sincerity in his eyes, and heard not a trace of false flattery in his tone. What he said sounded so genuine. So very romantic.

She didn't think twice about responding, "Why, thank you. Would you believe you're the most handsome, helpful man I've ever met?"

"Only if you say so." He looked pleased by her compliment, without any hint of vanity. "What say you take off your wet clothes?"

Terra hesitated, unsure whether to take his question at face value. On the one hand, he might be as upfront as he sounded, solely concerned about her well-being. On the other, he might be expecting more than verbal gratitude for his rescue effort.

"Hypothermia can be deadly," he prompted. "The same goes for pneumonia. Why risk your life again?"

Terra searched his face for signs of ulterior motives, but saw none. Or was she just letting his good looks and sex appeal override her good judgment?

"You'll have total privacy, of course."

"Promise?"

He crossed his heart. "On my honor as a Southern gentleman. I'll go up top while you change."

"All right." Somehow, she couldn't disbelieve him. "But I'll need some dry clothes."

"No problem." He returned to the bin and took out a sweatshirt as well as two pairs of sweatpants. "When you're ready, I'll fix you something hot to drink."

He went topside, taking a pair of the sweatpants with him. Terra hurried through the process of peeling off her waterlogged jeans, T-shirt and underwear.

She dried off, then put on the fleece-lined sweats. They had a subtle, intriguing male scent and dwarfed her figure, reminding her of her lifeguard's manly physique.

Rolling up the sleeves and trouser legs made them wearable, however, and something about the garments being his made her feel extrawarm and ultrafeminine.

She went to the cabin door and let him know the coast was clear. He came below, bare chested, wearing the other sweatpants. Once there, he paused to look her up and down.

"Beautiful," he murmured again. Then he blinked, as if shaking himself out of a daze. "Would you like some coffee, tea, cocoa? You name it."

"Cocoa, if it's not too much trouble."

"No trouble." He gestured at the captain's chair. "Have a ringside seat."

Terra curled into the chair, tucked her legs up under her and watched him set water to boil on a two-burner stove. He put instant mix into heavy mugs and added a splash of brandy to each one.

"You haven't told me your name," he said.

She decided that she wasn't really herself right then, and under the circumstances, her name was far more earthly and earthbound than she felt. Something about him made her feel as if she had suddenly become someone she'd never been before, someone she'd been saving within herself for a special occasion.

"I like the name you already gave me," she told him impulsively. "Mermaid."

He looked surprised and pleased, then intrigued. "Okay. So what's my name?"

"That's easy, Sailor."

"Fair enough." He grinned. "Sailor and Mermaid, the long-awaited sequel to *Splash!*"

Terra laughed, feeling comfortable, cozy and very much at home in the snug cabin. She felt as relaxed and natural as if she'd known him for years, and from what she could tell the feeling was mutual. Underlying it all was irresistible attraction, sexual awareness, ever-heightening anticipation.

It seemed to her that she'd leapt overboard into the ultimate romantic fantasy, complete with a sexy hero, provocative surroundings and intimate atmosphere. She felt as safe and protected as if she'd been imagining the whole thing.

Jilly and Fallon would never believe where she was right now or who she was with. The sailor. They'd turn crisp with envy if they could see her now.

She wondered if they'd noticed her absence yet. Probably not. More likely, they assumed she was finally throwing off her inhibitions with Greg or someone else in a bunk room on the houseboat.

"So, do you live around here?" the man asked, handing her a mug of steaming, brandy-scented chocolate.

She took a sip. "California. What about you? Your accent sounds local."

"It is. From one of the offshore islands, though, not Charleston. This is my last night in port. Come dawn, I'll put out to sea for the next few months."

His words shifted her imagination into high gear. She pictured him sailing the seven seas in pursuit of dangerous adventure and fabulous fortune. The image fit the fantasy, and led her to feel further and further removed from reality.

It was starting to seem long ago that she'd almost died. And almost died a virgin!

She told him, "Tomorrow, I leave, too. Back to the Golden State."

He gazed at her through the steam rising from his mug. "It's the last night for both of us, then."

She met his gaze and willingly let it take hold of her. There was no question in her mind what his thoughts were, or what his husky tone implied. His eyes said it all—that he desired her, that he'd be wonderful to her if she would stay with him tonight.

Terra found herself thinking, Yes, yes, yes. Her gaze dropped to the firm, sensual shape of his lips and prompted a relentless urge to kiss him, touch him, put her whole self in his hands. The man was perfect. So perfect that she wasn't tense. The mood was ideal, and for the first time in her life she wanted to be swept away.

If she didn't respond to him, and the plane crashed tomorrow, she'd die—as she'd almost died tonight—without ever experiencing a man like this.

"I don't want to go back to the party," she said.

"Good," he replied in a low, thrumming tone, "because I don't want you to go."

"Why not?"

"You know why, Mermaid. I'm not the only one here feeling, well, romantic." He paused. "Or am I?"

"No . . . not only you. It's so strong, and so much of a surprise."

He nodded. "The best surprise I've ever had, no exceptions."

"Me, too." She licked her lips. "Except, we barely know each other."

He agreed, "Barely. But it doesn't seem to matter, yoes it?"

"No. Nobody like you ever happened to me before."

"I feel the same about you. Are we dreaming, or what?"

"Maybe. If we are . . . I don't want to wake up."

"Neither do I. Not until morning." He put his mug down and silently moved toward her.

She set her own aside, too, and rose from the chair. As naturally as if she'd done it countless times before, she went into his arms, tipped her head back and whispered, "Make love to me, Sailor."

"I'll die if I don't," he whispered back.

"Me, too."

"Ahh, Mermaid, you're a dream come true."

She lifted her lips to his kiss and let romantic passion rule her last night of spring break. . . .

1

Five years later...

TERRA CAMDEN FROWNED at the produce basket full of rutabagas on her office desk. They were forcing her to hole up in her office and work late on Friday. All week long they'd been there, frowning back at her in their own, inert, turnipy way. By Wednesday, she'd begun referring to rutabagas as the R-word. Now, she was beyond words with frustration.

The restaurateur who'd sent them had hired her to redesign and rewrite his menus, which she'd done except for thinking up two tantalizing words—or three at most—that would sell a dinner entrée of roast beef and rutabagas to diners who wanted nothing to do with the undelectable R-word.

For the first time in her career, she questioned why she'd chosen to be a menu specialist. Someone whose professional aim was to attract, entice and seduce with words that had taste buds, so to speak.

"You're a dirt-poor rooting section," she grumbled under her breath at the rutabagas. "It's the best I can say for you."

Her secretary, Macy, buzzed her on the speaker phone and asked, "Are you inspired yet?"

"Brain-dead is more like it." Terra groaned.

"Want me to keep taking messages on your incoming calls?"

"It's time you went home, Macy. Past time."

"I'll think about it," Macy said, and rang off.

Terra scrutinized the rutabagas again and concentrated. Words. She needed just the right words of a specialized, suggestive language known as menu-ese in the food-service world. Creative menu copy, paired with an attractive format, could coax and cajole, manipulate and maneuver, titillate and tantalize. Unfortunately, every word and phrase in her professional vocabulary was failing her at the moment.

Her client ran an upscale Americana-style restaurant; her menu design, if she could solve the final problem it posed, would make the restaurant's cash register ring to the tune of higher profits.

Squinting at the basket, she wished its contents would bring a description better than Roasted Root Veggies to mind. She didn't want to take the problem home for the weekend. She wanted to solve it now. And the client wanted the sample menus first thing Monday morning!

Stumped for a solution, she stood from the desk and stretched out the kinks in her shoulders. Hearing Macy start up the copy machine, Terra went out to stop her. A skinny, wide-eyed, mop-top redhead, Macy was a go-getter. Too much of one today.

Terra chided her, "It's almost six, time for you to call it a week."

"I'm waiting for you to hit rutabaga pay dirt," Macy replied, turning off the copy machine.

"No chance. I'm not even close to a breakthrough."

"Maybe it'll come to you over the weekend."

"Not if the past week is any indicator of success," Terra said with a sigh. "It's times like this that I miss Aunt Claire more than ever."

Until a year ago, Camden Consulting had been Claire's business, a one-woman show in downtown San Francisco. Throughout high school and college, Terra had worked part-time for her, learning all that her aunt could teach her about menu design, food merchandising and copywriting. After college she went to work as a consultant with Claire.

Last year, Claire died in a traffic accident and left Camden Consulting to Terra. Terra had kept it successful, and loved the work, but she always missed Claire's expertise and guidance.

"I wish I had known her," Macy sympathized.

"She wouldn't have had any problem making rutabagas sound delicious," Terra said with a sad smile.

Macy wrinkled her nose. "They're the weirdest vegetables, except for gingerroots maybe."

"Weird," Terra agreed, "until you taste what a creative chef can do with them. Then they really do deserve to be served with pride and eaten with relish. But getting that across on a menu is no mean feat."

Macy pretended to gag. "They look like something even starving Pilgrims wouldn't have touched."

Terra brightened. "Pilgrims. That's an idea." She grabbed a pen and paper from Macy's desk and started scribbling. "Macy, bring up Synonymous on your computer. What's under *pilgrim?*"

Macy turned to the keyboard and activated the program. She read off the first few synonyms. "Crusader, devotee, tourist, colonist."

Terra jotted down the fourth word. "Keep going." She chewed thoughtfully on the pencil while Macy continued to the end of the listing.

". . . settler, pioneer, homesteader."

"Not colonial enough," Terra said, shaking her head.

"Terra, you just said it. Not Colonial Rutabagas, but what about Colonial Pot Roast?"

"Yes!" With a gleeful smile, Terra wrote it down. "It sounds cozy and comforting. Feel-good food. Bless you, Macy Medford."

"Not yet," Macy demurred. "The roots are still weird and nameless."

"True, but now they've got a concept going for them. Let's brainstorm . . . free-associate. The Pilgrims were colonials and what else?"

"Founding fathers."

"Hmm. Let's see now, as founding fathers they gave our country its history."

"Its past, its yesteryear," Macy said.

"Days of old," Terra responded. "Historical beginnings . . ." She shut her eyes to concentrate. "I'm on the verge of one, perfect, historical-sounding word." She popped her eyes open. "That's it!"

"What?"

"Heritage. Heritage Vegetables." Terra breathed a long sigh of triumph and relief.

Macy applauded. "Heritage even sounds healthy, for some reason," she said. "You're a genius, nothing less."

Terra put up a hand. "Without your own genius, I'd still be scraping the bottom of my brain. Thank you more than I can ever say."

"No, thank *you* for hiring me when nobody else would," said Macy.

Terra smiled, remembering the day a year ago when Macy had applied for the secretarial job. Five months pregnant, unwed and unemployed, Macy had been desperate for work.

"My lucky day," Terra assured her.

"Ours both," said Macy. "If I'd known then what I know now about my Venus and Mars, not to mention Saturn and Jupiter."

Terra wagged a finger at her. "As if your horoscope has anything to do with anything."

Astrology was always a subject of friendly debate between them. Whereas Macy put stock in stargazing, Terra believed that fate was determined by human behavior, not the solar system. Her own life for the past few years had certainly been the outcome of her own weaknesses and strengths, not planetary influences. Nevertheless, she found Macy's horoscopic forecasts amusing and entertaining.

"Either way, you gave me a hand up when I was down and out and I'll never forget it," Macy said gratefully.

Terra reflected that there was more that Macy would never forget—the sudden miscarriage that ended her unplanned pregnancy. Macy's situation, so similar in certain ways to Terra's own at one time, had forged a deep emotional bond between them.

A beep sounded from the fax machine and Macy took the message that came out. "Ooh, a love letter. To you from your favorite guy."

Taking the sheet of paper Macy handed her, Terra saw that it was covered by a big, lopsided, hand-drawn heart. "To Mommy from Josh," she read, a lump of happy, loving emotion forming in her throat.

All day long she'd looked forward to spending a quiet evening with her four-year-old son and her parents at their house. Her mother was both grandma and baby-sitter to Joshua.

For Terra, dividing time between Josh and Camden Consulting was a constant struggle. As sole provider for Josh and herself, she was always torn between him and her career.

Her blue-eyed, dark-haired son was a joy, the breath of her life. She found herself thinking wistfully, *If he had a father to send drawings to...* But that wasn't anywhere on the horizon. Her child's biological father would never know of his offspring, would never receive a heart full of love sent to Daddy from Josh.

Terra held a fading hope that Josh would have a stepfather someday, yet there wasn't time in her life lately for more than a casual date now and then. Besides that, she feared getting serious, since it would compel her to reveal the sordid secret that she'd conceived Josh during a one-night stand.

It hadn't seemed sordid on the night it happened, but shocking, tragic developments soon afterward had kept her silent about how and by whom she'd gotten pregnant. She alone knew the story.

For Josh's sake, she'd keep her silence forever about his father's identity.

Macy broke into her thoughts. "Where did Josh fax from?"

"My father's new machine. Mom gave it to him at Christmas, but Dad had a techno fear attack and put off installing it until last night. He—" The phone rang and she stopped as Macy answered it.

"Camden Consulting. Oh, hi. Fine, thanks, and you?"

Terra turned back toward her own office, but Macy motioned her to stay.

"Terra left just a moment ago," Macy fibbed. "Hold on a sec while I try to catch her." She pushed the hold button and told Terra, "It's Columbia. She's got a big menu project for you."

Columbia Hanes was a celebrity chef, Terra's top client and also her friend. After gaining great fame in San Francisco, Columbia had returned a few months ago to her birthplace in the South, where her African-American roots ran deep. She was now the executive chef at the luxurious, exclusive Bride's Bay Resort on Jermain's Island off the coast of South Carolina.

Terra had been expecting—and dreading—that Columbia would eventually want her to go there and work up new menus for the resort.

"Would you rather get back to her on Monday?" Macy asked.

"No, put her through on my line."

"Terra, are you okay?"

"Sure. Why?"

"You look like Columbia's project is the worst news in the world."

"I'm just root veggie'd out, that's all." She returned to her office and picked up the phone.

"Columbia, hi. What's happening?"

"Nothing you can't handle," the chef replied in her usual warm, friendly tone. "I need new menus all around—dining rooms, grill, banquets, catering, special events. In addition, there are some big VIP events coming up that I need menus for, too."

"Well, I'd love to work on it with you on everything, but—"

"Terra, please don't tell me you're booked too far ahead to help me out on short notice."

"I'm afraid so," Terra told her. "My calendar next week is full and after that I'm taking Josh on vacation for two weeks. When I return I—"

"Any chance you could make it a working vacation and spend it here?"

"Not unless I win the lottery. I mean, seriously, two weeks at a luxury resort is beyond my means."

"I can easily comp your stay, Terra. Room, meals, you name it, I'll comp it and pay your full fee, as well."

"That's very generous," Terra murmured, striving to think of several more reasons why she couldn't take on the work.

The truth she couldn't tell was that she had a connection to Jermain's Island and Bride's Bay Resort that no one else knew about. It was too tragic and painful for her to reveal to anyone. She'd never actually been to the island, but had a connection nonetheless, one that had to remain a secret.

"How *is* Josh, by the way?" Columbia asked.

"Oh, just great, having a ball in preschool. And how's Lalie?"

"Mama's going strong, still overjoyed that I'm back on home ground. 'Where I belong,' she says." Columbia chuckled. "She sends her best."

Terra and Claire had gotten to know Lalie Hanes quite well from the many times she'd visited her daughter in San Francisco. The four of them had often gotten together for lunch or dinner at those times, and when Claire died, Lalie came out from South Carolina for the funeral.

"Likewise from here," Terra said.

"You can tell her in person when you get here. In fact, come to think of it, Mama can baby-sit Josh for you a few hours each day. How's that for a bright idea?"

It was much too bright for Terra's comfort. "I'd hate to inconvenience Lalie."

"Trust me, she'd be thrilled."

Terra suppressed a sigh. "Columbia, can I get back to you on this next week?"

"Of course. First thing, if you can."

"Monday morning," Terra agreed. She hung up and went out to Macy's desk.

Macy was preparing to leave. "Anything I can do before I go?" Macy asked. "Like book you the next flight to South Carolina?"

"I'm not going, Macy."

"What?" Macy looked shocked. "Why?"

Terra reeled off all the reasons she'd given Columbia, adding that the chef had suggested a working vacation. "It's against my vacation rules, unfortunately. Josh deserves all of me on holiday, not part of me."

"What did Columbia say when you declined?"

"Well, actually, I didn't tell her no. I stalled her until Monday."

"No disrespect, Terra, but you're not acting anything like yourself."

"After a week of trying to wring charm out of rutabagas," Terra replied, faking a weary smile, "it's no wonder."

"Maybe not," Macy allowed. "But right now, *I* wouldn't turn down a big client. Or a working vacation at a posh resort on a romantic island. I'll bet your aunt would go for it if she could."

"True, but Aunt Claire wasn't a single mom." Terra shook her head. "I'll call next week and decline."

"Geez, Terra, I don't get this. You've never turned down work in the whole year I've been here. Especially not work for Columbia."

"Macy, I haven't taken a vacation since college and I'm not going to let business interfere in the one I've got planned."

Looking unconvinced and bewildered, Macy gathered up her raincoat and umbrella. "I'd better get going or I'll be late."

"For what?" Terra was eager to change the subject.

"A date, unbelievably, of the blind variety." Macy grimaced.

Terra had a moment of surprise, then gave Macy a thumbs-up. "Good for you."

"My social life needs something more than me going for it," Macy agreed dubiously, "but this?" She trudged to the door.

Terra could easily relate to Macy's apprehension about dating after a year of keeping to herself. It was good to see her stepping out and giving romance a wary chance. Macy had a lot to offer the right man.

In the doorway, Macy stopped and turned. "It seems to me we could rearrange next week's schedule so you could do the resort job then."

"That would effectively put me out of town for the next three weeks," Terra reasoned.

"You don't trust me to hold down the fort here that long?"

"Macy, *that* is the farthest thing from my mind. You're as essential to this business as I am."

Macy's dubious expression didn't change, so Terra decided to give her material proof. "Don't ask why, but please go to my computer and print out filename *Assist* from the *Admin* directory."

Looking perplexed, Macy put down the umbrella and went into the other office. Terra sat down in Macy's chair and thought back over the conversation with Columbia. If Columbia only knew what turmoil her call was causing.

The trouble was that Josh's father had been Rafe Jermain, a son of the family that owned part of the island, including Bride's Bay Resort.

On Jermain's Island off the coast of South Carolina, Rafe had grown to manhood. Terra often, unwillingly, pictured him as a young man on the island Columbia and Lalie had described. Time and again, she had visualized Rafe at the helm of a sleek, swift sloop, sailing the coastal waters, his blue eyes fixed on a distant horizon, his dark hair tousled by the wind.

Rafe's eyes... the same clear, deep blue as Josh's. The cleft in his chin... the same as Josh's. The same, the same...

Terra closed her eyes and sighed. Maybe she'd never get over Rafe, never shake off her conflicts about him. While half of her heart despised him, the other half clung to her intimate, erotic memories of him. He'd been her first lover, unforgettable for that alone.

A superb lover, she remembered, *sensitive and passionate and romantic.* She would never forget how special he had made her feel, how supremely desirable. Even now, despite her churning conflicts, the vivid memory of making love with Rafe was an unstoppable turn-on. Remembering was all it took to arouse her deepest desires and make her yearn to experience again the intense emotional and sexual pleasure he had given her.

It was impossible to forget Rafe's hot lips roving slowly over her body, his wet tongue stroking her nipples, his fingers sliding into the heat between her thighs. Gently, so gently, he had received the gift of her virginity and made that first time almost painless, perfectly wonderful. From midnight to dawn, she'd lost her head and reveled in passion with a perfect stranger....

Macy's return to the front office prompted Terra back to reality. She opened her eyes as Macy said, "You've got to be kidding."

"Kidding? Why?"

"It's a promotion offer."

"I know. I was saving it for your salary review next month. What do you think?"

Macy blanched. "About being your assistant?"

"You're ready to take a step up, Macy. Colonial Pot Roast is all the proof you need."

Macy backed away a step. "Wait a minute, wait a minute. I'm your secretary, not your— I mean, I'm not anywhere *near* ready to—"

"I know what you mean, and it's time you stop selling yourself short. You've learned a lot about this business in the past year."

"But, Terra, I've never gone to college, barely got through high school. You've got a degree, plus you worked here with your aunt all through school."

"I had advantages you've never had," Terra reminded her. "Parents and a stable home life, for instance, instead of a cot in an orphanage. And Aunt Claire left me a well-established, successful business."

"Which you've kept successful," Macy put in.

"Not without your help, Macy. You've overcome a lot of adversity and I feel you can go far with your quick mind and willingness to work hard."

"Terra, you just don't—"

"Furthermore, I know of a night-school scholarship that can be arranged for a promising candidate who shows talent and creativity."

Macy fell silent, looking wildly uncertain.

Terra turned Macy's own words on her. "Don't turn it down. Go for it. If you dare."

"What if I screw up?" Macy gulped. "What if I get it all wrong? What if I come up short?"

"You'll never know if you don't give it a go," Terra challenged. "This is your chance."

"Oh, brother, Terra. You're letting the Libra in you champion the underdog in me too much this time."

"I know you can do it."

"Well, *I* know *you* can do Bride's Bay. Why turn it down?"

"That's different."

"No, it's to die for, businesswise and funwise."

Terra shooed her through the door. "Quit nagging."

"Cheerleading," Macy corrected.

"Whatever, have fun tonight."

Macy looked doubly doubtful. "I'll try."

"Think over the offer this weekend," Terra said. "See you on Monday."

Macy gave a nervous wave, tucked the printout into her handbag and left. Terra locked the door and sat down in the silent office, wishing that she hadn't been such a starry-eyed romantic five years ago.

She had only herself to blame for the night of passion she shared with Rafe Jermain on his sailboat in Charleston Harbor. It had been a night out of time, a few hours in which she'd gotten carried away and ended up pregnant. There was no excuse for the costly mistake she had made with a handsome, fascinating stranger in the night. A man whose name she hadn't known while she was with him.

She would never have known his true identity if he hadn't become the biggest news of the decade soon after that night. And if Rafe had been a nobody instead of a Jermain, he would never have been headline news.

He wouldn't have become nationally known, infamous for betraying his country.

Her sweet, innocent Joshua—fathered by a traitor.

Never would Terra disgrace her son by revealing his father's identity. Nor would she humiliate her own parents, both retired army chaplains, with the revelation of their grandson's paternity. Her personal humiliation was all there would be, known only to her.

Rafe Jermain, missing and long-presumed drowned at sea, was her unspeakable shame and the shame of the patriotic Jermain family, as well. Terra felt for them with all her heart, aware of the pain it would cause them to know that Rafe had fathered a child on his last night in home port.

She wasn't acquainted with his family, although Columbia and Lalie were, but she knew the Jermains would never get over the scandal any more than she herself would. It gave her some comfort to know she wasn't alone in being ashamed of Rafe; there was no solace in bearing her burden all alone. The Jermains had one another. She had no one but herself.

Over the years, Terra avoided self-pity by keeping her mind focused on her son and her career—one day at a time. Now, though, her thoughts rushed back to the past and then raced forward to a possible future in which she and Josh would go to Jermain's Island and become acquainted with Josh's other family.

Just to meet them would be . . .

Terra halted the thought. To meet them would be pointless, she told herself. There wasn't any sense in it, or in becoming acquainted, except to . . .

No. Her own natural curiosity about the Jermain family was reason enough to decline Columbia's request. Nothing would be accomplished by going to Rafe's home. At the very least, it would be unwise. Upsetting. Painful.

She already had heartache for a lifetime, and then some.

She couldn't take on the job, no matter how good a client Columbia was or how friendly they'd been over the years. No matter how curious she'd always been about Josh's other family, she must resist the temptation to find out any more than she already knew.

Let the past alone, she warned herself. No matter what, she couldn't go to Bride's Bay!

2

TERRA SENT A REPLY fax to Josh, then locked up the office. Out on Market Street, she boarded a city bus that would take her to the modest Presidio neighborhood where her parents lived.

Once a U.S. army base where they had been stationed, the Presidio was now a recreational area. To Terra, the former base would always be where she had grown up, the only child of two army chaplains, Andrew and Hillary Camden.

Both were retired from the military now—her mother for the past few years, her father for the past few weeks. He had plans to start up a small, in-home, mail-order business to supplement their army pensions.

Terra gazed out of the bus window, wishing she'd been able to spare her parents the disappointment and heartache they'd felt when she became pregnant in the spring of her junior year at SFSU.

Shocked, yet supportive, they'd sustained her decision to keep and raise her child. At first, though, there were the inevitable questions: "How did this happen? Why? Were you forced? Who is the father?"

She would only tell them, "It was consensual. A terrible mistake. I'm responsible for the consequences. But please, don't ever think that you failed me. I failed myself and the values you taught me."

"People will be curious, Terra."

"Tell them I'm doing what's right for me and leave it at that."

"Very well, but . . . shouldn't the father know about this, whoever he is?"

"No. He wouldn't care, anyway."

Troubled and grieved by her situation, but determined to stand by her decision, they asked no further questions and kindly discouraged inquiries from curious friends and co-workers.

Several months later, Terra's child was born to their complete and total acceptance. Now, her family couldn't imagine life without Joshua Andrew Camden.

Joshua Andrew Jermain, an inner voice corrected her. It was a voice that wouldn't be silenced, wouldn't allow her to forget that Jermain blood ran in Joshua as surely as her own did.

"Last stop. End of the line." The bus driver's announcement brought her to her feet. Terra stepped out and walked two short blocks to her parents' house. Her apartment was conveniently nearby, a few blocks away, in the opposite direction.

Someday, she hoped to buy a house. Someday, after she'd saved up for Joshua's college education.

"Mommy!" He came running out of the front door before she reached the front step.

Terra scooped him up and hugged him tightly. Her father stood in the doorway, a lanky man whose kind, honest face inspired trust and respect. Her mom, nearly the same height as Andrew, was behind him, her slender arms circled around his waist. Hillary's luminous smile outshone the porch light.

"I faxed!" Josh crowed.

Terra smothered him with kisses. "So did I! Did you get mine?"

"Yep. And Macy's, too!" He wriggled out of her arms and tugged her toward the door.

"Macy?" she questioned, perplexed.

"Uh-huh. Come 'n' see."

"It transmitted just great," Andrew said. "My Christmas present works."

Hillary chided her husband gently, "High time, too. We can't run a mail-order business without a fax."

"We're not in business yet," he reminded her. "Terra's the only Camden in business right now."

Terra gave him and her mother quick hugs. "Macy faxed me here?"

"Nothing to be concerned about from the sound of it," Andrew said. "Just a few words." He moved toward his office. "I'll get it for you."

Josh protested. "I wanna, Grando."

"Okay. Save me the trip."

Josh raced away and came back with the message. He showed off his knowledge of the alphabet by spelling out Macy's name before handing the paper to Terra.

The message was brief. "I checked and your stars are *perfect* for the Bride's Bay job. Really, Terra, go for it!"

Aware that her father couldn't have helped reading it first, Terra folded the page and stuffed it into her coat pocket. As casually as possible, she shrugged out of the coat and made light of her secretary's encouraging words.

"Macy gets overexcited by the darnedest things at times. As if I put any belief in my stars."

Hillary took her coat from her. "Sit down and relax with Josh while Dad helps me finish cooking dinner."

Terra flopped gratefully into an armchair and Josh scrambled into her lap. He started telling her all the news of his day, beginning with preschool. Terra found herself only half listening, distracted by thoughts of South Carolina.

"I made a sailboat!" Josh enthused. His blue eyes— so like Rafe Jermain's—sparked with excitement. "A paper one. It floated in the sink. Then it sunk."

Terra murmured, "Poor boat."

Josh's words didn't help distract her from thoughts of Rafe, for Rafe had been a boating enthusiast. Her one and only encounter with him had been in Charleston Harbor on his sailboat. Six weeks later, his boat had sunk far out in the Caribbean near the island republic of Montinerro. He'd been smuggling arms to Montinerro's brutal dictator and been apprehended in the act by naval authorities. He tried to escape by going overboard into shark-infested waters and was never seen again.

Poor Josh, she thought. *He must never, never know.*

"Mommy?"

"Hmm?"

"Why don't we have a daddy?"

The words sank in and Terra caught her breath. She cleared her throat and managed to reply. "He's somewhere else."

So far, that vague answer had satisfied Josh whenever he'd questioned her about his male parent. Now, though, he was looking distrustful of her simple words.

"How come?"

"Let's talk about it tomorrow. Okay?"

"Steven's daddy is big. I want *my* daddy."

Steven was one of Josh's classmates at preschool, she recalled worriedly. It was natural for Josh to start comparing himself to other children and noticing a difference.

"How big is Steven's father?" she inquired, hoping to divert him. Maybe he wouldn't ask again soon. Maybe she'd figure out what to say in the meantime. "As big as a dinosaur?"

Josh's eyes grew round, and Terra thanked heaven that his imagination was active and his sense of adventure easily tapped.

"*I* can beat up a T-Rex," he stoutly announced, flexing his biceps to prove his strength.

"Josh, what big muscles you're growing."

He puffed up with pride and abruptly changed the subject. "I wanna be a sailor, okay?"

Troubled by his wish, she murmured, "We'll see."

A moment later he wiggled out of her lap and went to display his muscles to his grandfather. Terra closed her eyes and wondered what to say the next time he popped the daddy question. The answer refused to come.

She only knew that she couldn't tell him the truth. He was too young to understand why and how she'd gotten pregnant in her junior year at college.

Thinking back to that time in her life, she recalled her two free-spirited dormmates, Jilly and Fallon. The day before spring break, they impulsively decided to go somewhere like Fort Lauderdale for the first big weekend of the college holiday.

Terra happened to mention another place she'd heard was popular at spring break—Myrtle Beach, South Carolina. In fact, she'd heard it from her aunt's famous client, Chef Hanes, a native South Carolinian. That was recommendation enough for Jilly and Fallon. They decided on Myrtle Beach and urged Terra to join them.

She remembered how reluctant she'd been to go. Her life before college had been sedate and sheltered, regimented somewhat by military regulations. Overly protective, her parents had put her in private girls' schools in San Francisco. Not until college did she have social autonomy, and even then she didn't begin to break out of her mold until Jilly and Fallon moved into the dorm. Dramatic-arts majors, they were spontaneous, free-spirited, sexually experienced and adventurous.

If they hadn't talked her into it, she would never have gone. And if she had never gone, she'd have no problem about going to that area now.

"Sweetpea?"

Terra opened her eyes and blinked. "What?"

"Sorry to wake you, but dinner's five minutes away."

She rubbed her eyes and fibbed to her father, "I dozed off. What a week it's been. Busy."

"Sounds like you'll be busier," he said, settling his tall frame onto the sofa, "if Macy's fax means you're wanted over at Bride's Bay Resort."

"Wanted," she confirmed hesitantly, "but not willing to take on the project."

Andrew blinked at her. "Not willing? Did Chef Hanes quit working there or something?"

"No. It, well, just doesn't fit into my schedule."

Her father looked all the more surprised. "Your best-known client doesn't fit into your schedule? Claire would turn over in her grave if she could hear you."

"Dad, I just can't drop everything else and go."

"Claire would have worked out a way," he said. "Sweetpea, this isn't like you at all, turning down business." He paused. "What's wrong? You seemed worried when you got home, and you still do."

Terra was well aware of how difficult it was to deceive either of her parents about her moods and motives. They'd always been overly protective of her, ultrasensitive to every nuance of her behavior. She couldn't really blame them since she was their only child, all they had. She'd always understood how precious she was to them, and being a parent herself now gave her an even deeper understanding of their concerns.

"I'm dizzy with relief," she told him. "The rutabagas had me on the ropes."

"If you say so," he acceded reluctantly. "But if there's something else . . ."

"Nothing at all, Dad." She saw him looking only half-convinced. "Look, I know I can come to you and

Mom, no matter what the trouble. Not that there's any trouble."

He said, "Losing Columbia Hanes as a client would be troublesome, not to mention straining your friendship with her. There must be some way you can pull it off, maybe postpone your vacation plans."

Terra reluctantly explained that Columbia had suggested a working vacation.

"Sounds reasonable," Andrew said, nodding.

"It wouldn't be fair to Josh, Dad. He deserves the entire time with me, not part of it."

Andrew shrugged. "I don't know. Travel out of state would do him good at his age. What a geography lesson he'd get—and you would, too, for that matter."

"Dinner's on!" Hillary called from the kitchen.

Terra got up out of the chair, determined not to let her father's opinion shake her resolve. But then he made one final comment that blew her resolve to bits.

"Claire put her heart and soul into Camden Consulting," he said. "She never disappointed a client and I'd hate to see you disappoint one of her all-time favorites. You owe Claire nothing less than your best effort."

"MOMMY, ARE WE THERE?"

"Not quite. This is Charleston," Terra replied. She had Josh by the hand as they passed through the airport arrival gate. "Someone is supposed to meet us here, remember? He'll take us on a boat to the island."

Columbia had promised that the resort's marina manager would be there. Terra was expecting Kent Prescott, an athletic-looking "bachelor with a killer smile," as the chef had described him.

Terra saw him right away, a tall and muscular man with brown hair and hazel-green eyes. He was wearing a white windbreaker with the Bride's Bay logo stitched on the front.

"Ms. Camden?" he inquired.

"Yes, you're Mr. Prescott?"

"Kent," he said. "Welcome to South Carolina."

"Thank you. I'm Terra, and this is my son, Josh." She drew him forward.

"Hi, sir," Josh said.

As Prescott looked down at Josh, Terra couldn't help feeling a little apprehensive. She wondered if he had known Rafe, and if so whether he'd notice the resemblance. But he didn't even blink as he greeted her son.

"Hi, Joshua." He gave the boy a manly handshake. "How did you like your plane ride?"

Josh smothered a yawn. "Okay. Except I fell asleep." He glanced around. "Where's the boat?"

"First, we'll claim your luggage. Then I'll drive you and your mother to the dock."

Terra put her fears on hold as she and Josh followed Kent's lead to baggage claim. Along the way, Josh plied him with questions about the boat. Kent patiently answered in simple terms, describing a spacious, motor-powered cruiser with a comfortable passenger cabin.

While waiting at the luggage carousel, Terra chatted with Kent about his job and learned that he was a long-time friend of the Jermain family.

"Long enough that they trust me to manage their marina," he said, "which I'm more than happy to do."

He gave her the smile Columbia had described. Terra suspected it brought him above-average success with women. She couldn't picture him as a Don Juan, however; he seemed too well-mannered and low-key. More likely, women eagerly pursued him and he had his pick.

Terra found him very attractive, though not in any romantic sense. Unfortunately, that was the case with every man she met, no matter who. Something vital, something essential, was always missing. That is, ever since Rafe Jermain.

The Rafe she had known wasn't an infamous traitor, but a dashing seafarer who had dark hair, blue eyes and an aura of romantic intrigue about him.

Her preoccupation with him would have to stop, she told herself. It was morbid, perverse, useless and unproductive. If she didn't keep a tighter rein on the best memories of Rafe, sexual frustration would be her constant companion. It was unwelcome enough company as it was.

Fortunately, a distraction arrived in the form of the luggage, and Kent loaded it into a minivan. Driving out of the airport, he asked, "Have you two been to South Carolina before?"

"Nope," Josh replied. "Never ever."

Kent told him, "I guarantee you'll like it."

Josh looked doubtful. "I gotta have a baby-sitter."

"Well," Kent said, "you couldn't have a better one than Lalie Hanes."

Terra had some doubts of her own about Lalie's willingness to baby-sit Josh. Lalie had called to assure her it wouldn't be an inconvenience, but she hadn't sounded entirely enthusiastic. Maybe she'd just had a bad day when she called, Terra thought hopefully. But it wasn't easy to picture upbeat Lalie in a blue mood.

Kent added to Josh, "Her minifarm will be fun for you."

In the past, Lalie had described the small specialty farm. It supplied the resort with herbs, flowers and gourmet greens. Terra was familiar with similar mini-farms in the San Francisco area, where quality designer produce was a major issue among fine-dining chefs. Some growers had a cultlike following among the top chefs.

"Is Lalie fun?" Josh asked Kent.

Kent assured him of that and kept the conversational ball rolling between them. Before long, Josh was telling him all about the plane ride, the airline meal and how his ears popped during takeoff and landing. Terra kept silent, using the time to reorganize her apprehensions and the contents of her briefcase.

"Mommy, look! Boats!"

Kent was making a turn into a marina parking lot somewhere in Charleston Harbor. The lot and the sizable marina it served seemed vaguely familiar to her as she glanced around, perhaps because she'd been there before? Maybe she had, maybe not. All of the marinas she'd ever seen looked pretty much alike. Moreover, some details of that night five years ago had never been clear in her mind.

Kent parked the van, and when he came around to help her out, she asked, "Are there more marinas in the harbor?"

"Several," he replied, "including the municipal one."

He unloaded the luggage with the help of a dock employee, and Terra and Josh followed them into the mooring area. It harbored a variety of watercraft, ranging from small sailboats and houseboats to yachts.

Terra left off puzzling any further about details she couldn't recall. It was best not to know for sure, she decided, for what good would it do to be certain of exactly where it had happened that night?

She squeezed Josh's hand. "What do you think of our vacation so far?"

"Wow." He craned his neck to look up at the tall mast of a bobbing boat. "There's a million boats."

"At the very least," she agreed with an indulgent smile.

Walking along with him, Terra put off thoughts of the past. She switched to enjoying the sunny spring warmth in the salt air, the buoyant sight of sea gulls and pelicans soaring overhead, the expression of delight on Josh's face.

Kent took them down a wood-plank walkway to the cruiser he'd described earlier. Painted spotless white with gleaming teak trim and embellished with the resort's navy blue logo, it had an air of understated elegance and luxurious comfort.

"All aboard the *Indigo Moon*," Kent invited.

He showed them into the blue-upholstered passenger cabin, gave them life vests to wear and cold sodas to drink, then offered them a choice between riding in the cabin or up top at the helm with him.

For Josh, there was no question of where to ride. "On the top."

Terra agreed, so they went up with Kent to the upper half-deck where they took seats behind him. He cast off and steered the boat into the main harbor waterway.

Josh was beside himself, twisting around to take in all the sights.

"We're passing through historic Charleston Harbor," Kent told them. "Ahead is Fort Sumter, where the first shot of the Civil War was fired."

Terra settled back and watched her son's expressive face while Kent continued pointing out pertinent sights.

He recounted Charleston's early history, how it had been founded by European noblemen who had established great plantations on the coast and some of the coastal islands.

"Jermain's Island," he added, "was once a plantation."

Terra knew all that, and much more about the island, from nationwide news accounts of Rafe's treachery five years ago. Little about him and his illustrious family background had gone unreported by the major news media when he became a scandal.

Had the Jermain family not been prominent—politically, economically and socially—since pre-Civil War days, there would have been no shock value in the story. No media frenzy to report the crime. No avid public curiosity about the criminal. No field day for the news media.

Rafe had been characterized as the rogue of his upstanding family. Reporters described his love of high-seas adventure, told of how it had led him to drop out of college against his family's wishes. He'd gone sailing the world over, ostensibly on import-export business, and gained a reputation for having the wind in his mainsail and a babe in every port. In Charleston, he'd been known to associate with shady, unsavory characters who were rumored to be drug dealers or illegal arms traders, maybe both.

Terra still wasn't sure how much of it to believe. She tended more to trust in Columbia's reaction to the scandal. After all, Columbia knew him well and Lalie had practically raised him.

"I don't care how it looks," Columbia had stoutly maintained, "Rafe would never betray his country. I'll believe in him to my dying day, and so will my mother."

Terra came back to attention as she realized that Kent was speaking directly to her.

"You'll notice a lot of security equipment being installed at the resort," he was saying. "It's to upgrade the existing system for a diplomats' conference that's coming up a couple of weeks from now."

"I saw a news article about it," she recalled. "Something to do with a trade agreement between the U.S. and the Caribbean, isn't it?"

"Right. Some employees are suspicious of the extra surveillance going in at the resort, but management says it's necessary for everyone's safety. Employee background checks are twice as rigorous now."

"I wonder if I'm considered a part-time employee for the next two weeks," she said.

"I wouldn't be surprised if you've already been checked out. By the way, there's a rumor that the President and First Lady might vacation at the Bride's Bay next month."

"Really? That's exciting."

He nodded. "Just a rumor, though. I haven't noticed the Secret Service infiltrating the resort yet." He gave her a half teasing, half speculative look over his shoulder. "Unless you're an agent disguised as a menu consultant."

"Me?" Terra laughed. "Menus are my specialty, nothing more. Ask Columbia and Lalie, who've known me quite a while."

Kent smiled and shrugged. "I guess I'm still paranoid from when federal agents were all over the resort five years ago."

Terra managed not to skip a beat as she responded, "You mean what happened with Rafe Jermain."

"It was a tough time," Kent said. "The resort and the entire Jermain family lost all security credibility for almost a year afterward, and there was no telling the hotel guests and the FBI apart. One way or another, everybody on the island was investigated for ties to the incident."

"How are things now?" Terra inquired. Casually, she hoped.

"Back to normal, at least for the resort. For everyone who knew Rafe, though, particularly his family, it's still painful."

Keeping a steady tone with effort, she said, "Not everyone believes he was guilty, from what Columbia and Lalie have mentioned."

"The vast majority thinks he was."

"What's your own opinion, Kent?"

"Innocent, despite all the evidence to the contrary. And yours?"

"Undecided."

Josh interrupted, tugging her sleeve. "Can I drive the boat, Mommy?"

"That's up to Kent."

"Fine with me," Kent said.

Terra gave Josh permission, and Kent took the boy under his wing at the wheel. She had to resist an instinctive desire to snatch her child back and keep him close at her side. He should have this golden opportunity to interact with a man younger than her father.

Watching her son gaze up admiringly at the skipper, Terra was uncomfortably aware of how much Josh missed without a male parent in his life. There was also the discomfiting awareness of how much she herself missed without a partner.

She tried to picture herself with Kent, yet somehow couldn't see it. Despite being likable and good-looking, he wasn't right. Not the way Rafe had been that one special night, before she found out who he really was.

Once again, she found her thoughts dwelling on him. Again, she made herself leave off and focus on the present. What a beautiful day it was. What an exhilarating boat ride. What a treat for Josh.

She held that positive mind frame for the rest of the half-hour trip to the island.

"MOMMY, LOOK!"

She caught her first glimpse of Jermain's Island, which loomed, lush and spring green, on the eastern horizon. Rafe's home turf, Terra thought. His birthplace. His nameplace.

"Land, ho," Kent said. "Five miles wide and three miles long, shaped sort of like an ear." He pointed to the northern shore. "The village is there, as well as several private estates. The south end is a forest preserve with trails for equestrians and hikers. The resort fills up the middle."

Terra had an island map that Columbia sent to her. It added detail to Kent's comments, and also listed the resort's world-class amenities: antique-furnished guest rooms, golf and health clubs, tennis, Olympic-size pool, shooting range, riding stables, five-star restaurant.

Kent brought the *Indigo Moon* into Bride's Bay and proceeded to a small marina where a variety of watercraft were moored. Inland from the marine stood the hotel, an elegant, white-brick mansion with stately columns. Encircled by immaculate lawns and graced by a formal garden, it was a breathtaking sight.

"Oh, my," Terra murmured. "It's magnificent."

Her attention drew away to three people at the dock. She recognized Columbia, a statuesque, African-American woman dressed in a traditional chef's uniform and a high, white toque. Lalie stood next to her—stout, gray-haired and casually dressed. She had a soccer ball in one hand.

Apparently a gift for Josh, Terra thought. The third person was a tall man of robust build with thick, curly white hair, dressed in the livery-style uniform of a doorman or porter. They all smiled and waved as Kent docked the boat. Once it was secure at its berth, Terra stepped onto the dock with Josh.

The two women greeted them with glowing smiles and warm hugs. Lalie gave Josh the ball, to his great delight.

"I'm all ready for you to come over this evening for dinner," she said. She winked at Josh. "I hope you like chocolate-chip cookies for dessert."

Josh nodded enthusiastically. "Can I bring my ball?"

"You surely can."

He hugged it to his chest. "Thanks, ma'am."

Terra saw that no one seemed to notice Josh's resemblance to Rafe. She didn't think it was all in her own mind, yet nobody so far had even blinked. Or was the liveried gentleman doing a double take?

Terra judged him to be in his late sixties. His weathered, darkly tanned face creased into a puckish smile as he caught her glance, and his piercing blue eyes sparked with spry, wily mischief. That and a gold hoop earring in his left ear suggested a colorful, possibly eccentric personality.

He stepped forward and gave a jaunty bow. "Welcome, ma'am and young man. I'll see to your luggage for you."

Columbia introduced him as Shadroe Teach, the bell captain, adding that he knew everything about the resort and everyone there. He affirmed that she was right, and then disappeared into the boat.

Josh gazed up at Columbia. "What's on your hat?"

Columbia touched the small, fresh orchid pinned to her toque. "That's my trademark. Mama grows orchids in her greenhouse."

Leaving Shad to deliver the bags in a minivan, they walked to the hotel through the garden. There were box hedges, early-blooming roses, fragrant beds of alyssum and lavender, colorful azaleas and huge live oaks dripping with Spanish moss. Josh trotted ahead on the garden path, bouncing his new ball.

Terra breathed in the warm, fragrant air. "It's another world here. Lovely."

"And extremely busy beneath the serene, restful surface," Columbia said. "I'd planned to visit with you and Mama tonight, but one of my sous chefs came up sick and now I can't break away the rest of the weekend. So enjoy yourself until Monday morning."

Terra asked, "What time?"

"Oh, say nine to eleven in the morning, and maybe three to four in the afternoon."

They reached the hotel and went up the steps that led to the front veranda and the main door. Before going in, Terra took the ball from Josh so there'd be no breaking anything, especially not the splendid floor-to-ceiling windows that flanked the front doors.

Columbia showed them into a spacious lobby with pale yellow walls and polished wood floors. There was a long front desk and a glorious, sweeping staircase that made Terra think of Scarlett O'Hara at Twelve Oaks. It was no effort imagining a distant past when the mansion was host to socials, parties and balls—replete with Southern belles and gallant swains.

Yet, entering the mansion with Columbia who strode in like a queen—tall and regal, confident and charismatic—Terra was aware that life had been far from gracious, hospitable and romantic for the slave population in the old days. There would always be two sides to the complex history of the Old South.

"See what you would have missed if you'd gone somewhere else for a vacation?" Columbia said.

"I see," Terra assured her, nodding and smiling as if she wouldn't give the world to be somewhere else.

Anywhere else but here, she thought, unnerved to be on Rafe Jermain's home turf. And with his son, at that!

3

TERRA SIGNED IN at the front desk, then Columbia took them upstairs to their room. Located at the near end of the west wing, it was a spacious, pale pink chamber furnished with an antique four-poster, a trundle bed and a cozy Victorian love seat

Above the white marble fireplace hung a gilt-framed mirror, and on the mantel stood a vase of fresh, fragrant blooms. Next to the big, high bed was a charming step stool with a needlepoint cushion. A pair of French doors led out to a veranda that was enclosed by black wrought-iron railings.

Delighted, Terra said, "Columbia, thank you. It's wonderful."

The chef grinned. "It's nothing compared to my cuisine. Which reminds me, you're invited to dinner tomorrow night by Elizabeth Jermain and her husband, Judge Cameron Bradshaw.

"Miz Elizabeth owns the hotel, although her granddaughter, Liz, runs it. And Judge is retired from the bench." She added, "Josh is invited, too, of course."

"We'll look forward to it." Terra quaked inside at the prospect of meeting Rafe's grandmother and step-grandfather. "What time and where?"

"At seven, in their own suite at the far end of this wing. For your other meals, there's the main dining room, or the beach grill, or room service—as you wish." Columbia leaned out the door and looked down the hall. "Here comes Shad with your bags. Anything else you need, give me or the concierge a holler. Joanie Griffin, she's a whiz."

"Will do." Terra motioned her to go. "Don't waste any more valuable time on us. We'll get settled in and then go to Lalie's."

"If she doesn't answer the front door, she'll be out back in the gardens or the greenhouses. You remember the directions there?"

Terra quickly repeated them and reminded Columbia of the map. "Now, go. Get. Shoo."

"Thanks for understanding, Terra." The chef hastened away.

Shad came in with the luggage. He demonstrated how to work the locks, light switches and other controls, and chuckled over Josh's fascination with the old-fashioned bathroom fixtures. Terra wanted to tip him for his service, but he politely declined.

"Add it to the little lad's allowance," he said. With a wink and a jaunty salute, he went out whistling and closed the door.

Terra unpacked and ran a bubble bath for Josh. "I want you nice and clean for dinner and Lalie," she told him.

Once he was in the tub, playing with the inflatable bath toys she'd brought for him, Terra flopped on the big bed to unwind.

She wasn't sure what to think so far, as none of her fears had materialized. No one had looked twice at Josh, except for Shad perhaps. Maybe it was all in her own mind, or maybe vivid blue eyes were as common around here as seawater.

Rafe's eyes hadn't seemed at all common the night she met him. It would never have happened if not for Jilly and Fallon. They had been the catalysts, Terra remembered ruefully. And she had been foolish enough to let them influence her.

Jilly used to say, "You've been a good soldier too long, Terra Camden. Be a rebel for a change."

Fallon always chimed in, "Take some risks, pull out your stops, fracture a few rules."

Their friendly, relentless ribbing got under Terra's skin that year. They led her to question why she'd never rebelled against authority, rarely misbehaved, always lived up to expectations and got straight-A grades. What a geeky army brat!

So when spring break rolled around, she was prime for an escapade. It helped that her parents were away at a week-long chaplains' retreat and wouldn't know what she did. It also helped that Jilly had access to a frequent-flier account and finagled three free plane tickets. Before Terra could talk herself or her friends out of it, they'd all bleached their hair and flown to South Carolina.

She hadn't imagined that the escapade would result in motherhood for her . . .

The sound of Josh's voice brought her back from her memories. "Mommy, I'm all clean."

Terra went to get him dried off and dressed, then changed out of her traveling clothes into twill walking shorts, a sleeveless blouse and sneakers. She packed a small tote with Josh's nap blankie and some storybooks. He took charge of the soccer ball after solemnly promising he'd only kick it outdoors.

The walk to Lalie's house led through the village. Small and unpretentious, it had shops and services for the residents and resort guests, but no trendy boutiques. It had its own small marina and mariners' supply, a grocery and a general store that advertised a wide selection of books. Ye Olde Sandwich Shoppe looked quaint and charming, with blue-and-white checked curtains in the windows.

The route took them beyond the village to where the estates were located along the shore. They found that Lalie's minifarm was a sheltered strip of property between two grand estates. Her roomy stone cottage stood behind a high evergreen hedge, and as Columbia had said might happen, the doorbell went unanswered.

So they went to the back, where there were three compact greenhouses, several small plots of vegetable greens in various stages of growth and a wide lawn. Thick hedges on either side of the estate boundaries screened the little farm from the bigger homes.

The hedge on one side had a neighborly opening and Terra saw that the latticed gate was open.

She told Josh, "Maybe Lalie went next door for a minute. Let's kick your ball around on the lawn till she comes back."

Sure enough, Lalie came hurrying through the gate a few minutes later.

"I'm sorry I wasn't here," she said. "The Hamiltons next door are away on a long trip and I watch over their house when they're gone. Air it out, take in their mail and so forth."

"That's okay," Josh said, balancing the ball on his head. "We played."

The telephone started ringing an outside bell and Lalie threw up her hands. "Wouldn't you know I took my portable phone inside. If that's my sister in Germany, she won't want to talk to my message machine." She hurried toward the house. "Keep on playing. I'll be back."

"Take your time," Terra called after her.

Josh rolled the ball on the grass and they set to kicking it back and forth again. He had a strong kick for his age and size, so strong that he quickly booted it wild and it rolled through the open gate.

Chasing after it, they both paused in the gateway as the ball went down a long, gently sloping expanse of lawn on the other side. Beyond the end of the slope stood a big, beautiful, luxury home.

Josh's ball rolled all the way down and stopped at the edge of a brick patio. A set of French doors connected the patio to the house and Terra saw that they stood partly open, lined with sheer curtains that were billowing out on the breeze.

Terra made Josh stay at the gate, then jogged down over the wide lawn to retrieve the ball. Scooping it up, she paused, tempted to cross the patio and peek in through the doorway. Not to snoop, but just steal a glimpse at how the very rich lived. Too curious to resist the opportunity, she scampered across the bricks and drew the blowing curtains aside to peer inside.

She looked into a spacious bedroom where a carved-teak bed and sitting area were the focal points. The decor carried out a dramatic nautical theme, with models and paintings of historic sailing vessels.

Looking up, she saw that the ceiling was a fresco of a blue-black night sky spangled with stars and a crescent moon—perhaps a navigational map of the heavens.

Strangely, though, the bed was unmade and looked slept in. Stranger still, she heard a shower running in what she judged to be an adjoining bathroom. She could understand why the patio doors were open, since Lalie had said she aired the house, but why was the shower turned on?

Terra stepped into the bedroom and went to the half-closed door. A slight mist of soap-scented steam wafted out as she pushed the door all the way open and entered a spacious bathroom.

Looking around, she saw a hot-tub spa, a conventional bathtub, a separate shower with a frosted-glass door. Through the frosted door, a moving form was visible.

Shocked, she realized someone was in there. Someone tall with dark hair. Suddenly, before she could think any further, the shower spray stopped. The glass door sprang open.

A man stepped out. A man she knew!

Terra gasped and dropped the soccer ball, astonished by who she saw. She'd recognize him anywhere, anytime, with no doubt about his identity.

Too stunned to move, she gasped, "Rafe!"

He stared back with startled blue eyes, then grabbed a towel against his loins.

"Who are you?" he demanded.

His voice made her gulp. The compelling sound was unmistakable.

"R-Rafe Jermain," she stammered disjointedly.

"What do you want?"

She was too dumbfounded to form a reply, or even recall her own name. She couldn't move, couldn't breathe, couldn't believe her own eyes.

Suddenly her head swam, her ears rang and the bathroom carpet seemed to rise like a tidal wave under her feet.

Aghast, she thought, *I'm going to faint.*

Then, for the first time in her life, she did.

THE NEXT THING Terra knew, she was lying faceup on the teak bed. Two faces, Lalie's and Rafe's, looked down at her. She felt a cool, wet cloth on her forehead, a soft, satiny bedspread beneath her body.

She reached a trembling hand to her forehead. "Wh-what happened?"

"You passed out," Lalie said.

Terra blinked at Rafe with disbelief, then looked around for someone else. "Where is Josh?"

"Right outside," Lalie replied. "I told him you had to use the bathroom in here."

Hearing the ball bounce on the patio, Terra felt a bit calmer, although she couldn't believe her eyes about Rafe.

He spoke to Lalie. "He must be wondering what's taking so long."

"I'll go reassure him," she said, squeezing Terra's hand before slipping out through the French doors.

Meeting Rafe's blue gaze, Terra shook her head in confusion. "You're alive?"

"More or less," he replied guardedly. "Sorry I gave you a scare."

"You can't be real." She rubbed her eyes. "It doesn't make sense."

Lalie slipped in again and returned to the bed. "Josh is curious, but he's keeping busy with his ball." She leaned closer. "How are you feeling now?"

"Still a little faint."

Rafe asked, "When did you last eat a square meal?"

Terra recalled skipping lunch on the plane. "Breakfast, I guess."

"No wonder you dropped over," Lalie said. "You must be starving."

Glancing from Lalie to Rafe, Terra inquired uncertainly, "What's going on? Or am I hallucinating?"

Rafe and Lalie exchanged glances and Lalie nodded her head at him. Rafe answered reluctantly, "You're seeing straight."

"I don't believe it," Terra murmured. She shut her eyes, opened them again and found that he remained visible. "It's impossible."

Lalie patted her hand comfortingly. "After Rafe explains, you'll understand."

"Explains?" he questioned, giving Lalie an incredulous look. "As if she's going to believe me."

Lalie gave him a stern look in return. "*I* believe you. And knowing Terra, I hope she will, too. Besides, what choice do you have now?"

"One," he countered. "I get out of here, fast."

"And go where?" Lalie inquired. "Not very far, as recognizable as you are. Besides, how long do you think your hurt knee and back will hold up if you're on the run?"

"They might get me far enough away not to get caught."

"What about your internal bruises?"

"I'll tough them out."

"No, you'll undo all the good I've done healing you up these past two months."

"Look, I'm not going to stand still and get turned over to the feds."

Terra followed their dispute right and left, like a spectator at a tennis tournament. It was sinking in that Rafe wasn't a trick of her mind, nor a ghostly illusion. From what she saw, he was as alive as she and Lalie were. Astoundingly alive, although leaner and paler than she remembered from before. His eyes appeared to be a deeper blue now. Or maybe not, since she had never seen him in full daylight.

He apparently didn't recognize her, thank God. Maybe because her hair was natural brown and chin length now instead of long and surf-babe blond. Her body had matured, too, from pregnancy and nursing Josh. Aside from that, he probably had only the dimmest memory of her, if he even remembered her. To be sure, she hadn't marked the milestone in his life that he had marked in hers.

Lalie didn't give up quizzing him. "Who's going to nurse your jungle fever every time it crops up?"

"One way or another, I'll manage," Rafe countered grimly.

"You're only partly healed, Rafe Jermain. You've got healing yet to do."

"My health won't improve in federal custody. No one's going to believe I was framed."

Lalie shook her head. "Explain first and see."

He went silent, giving Terra a sidelong, suspicious look.

Terra was finally able to trust her eyesight, but she couldn't believe her ears. Perplexed, she questioned Rafe. "Did you say 'framed'?"

"Absolutely." His mouth made a cynical downturn. "But with no proof, what good is the truth?"

Lalie put in, "He's been too sick until now to prove what he needs to. He—"

Rafe interrupted curtly, "Don't bother explaining. It's useless."

"I'll bother till I'm blue in the face," Lalie informed him, shaking an authoritative finger for emphasis. "I'm your spiritual guardian, young man, and don't you forget it."

He put up his hands in defensive appeal. "I'm not forgetting. I'm just—"

"Then do me the favor of telling Terra what happened. She can decide where she stands after she hears you out."

Rafe appraised the woman who had innocently stumbled across him, who now had the power to expose him. She was beautiful—a slim, fine-figured, brown-eyed brunette—and he'd far rather just look his fill at her than waste breath on a true story she wouldn't believe. Shrewd judge of character that he was, he'd already decided she looked much too honest and law-abiding to give a known traitor any benefit of the doubt.

Nevertheless, he couldn't reject his godmother's impassioned appeal. She loved him as she loved her own family, and hadn't hesitated to harbor him when he'd dragged himself to her back door, half-drowned.

So, okay, he'd tell Terra Camden the facts. It wouldn't matter what she did or didn't believe because he knew she'd ultimately do what was best for her little boy. Now that she was an eyewitness to a federal crime—conspiracy—she'd call the feds. If she didn't, she'd risk being arrested and prosecuted. She'd never want the boy to have a mom in prison.

Lalie obviously hadn't considered the maternal angle yet. As always, her stouthearted belief was that truth would triumph, justice would prevail, faith and hope and love would conquer all.

Well, Rafe knew the world of covert operations didn't work that way. Only out of respect to Lalie would he tell Terra the truth as he knew it. Then, he'd get out and make damn sure his trail didn't lead back to his godmother.

He leveled a couldn't-care-less gaze on Terra. "If you'll listen, fine. If not, fine."

She gave his offer some long moments of grave thought, and during that time he assessed her again. He thought of how long it had been since he'd had a woman. Not since the night before he sailed out of Charleston Harbor five years ago. He'd never forget the woman or the night of passion he'd spent with her on his sailboat.

Unlike Terra, she had been blond, with wavy long hair that reached to her waist. Her eyes had been the softest, sexiest brown, a lot like Terra's. Or maybe not a lot, since he'd never seen his blond lover in daylight. There had only been that one night, so long ago.

Too long ago, which was one explanation for the painful, avid, sexual interest he'd taken in Terra from the moment she first gasped his name. He couldn't help but imagine himself alone with her in the bed where she lay.

Her softly rouged lips looked inviting, her feminine curves alluring, and it was all he could do not to stare at her like what he was—a man who hadn't had sex for years.

At the same time, though, there was something else about her that captured more than his sexual interest. He couldn't identify exactly what, but it made him feel protective, even romantic, and surprised at himself for feeling that way about a woman he didn't know.

Finally, Terra spoke, with a reluctance he could see and hear.

"All right," she said slowly. "I'll come back after dinner. Whatever you have to say, I'll listen."

Rafe couldn't hide his surprise that Terra had agreed to hear him out. *Waste of my good breath*, he told himself again.

Lalie beamed. "Bless you, Terra. I'll go tell Josh you won't be much longer in here." She hurried out the door.

Rafe took one of Terra's hands to help her off the bed. "Take it easy, now," he advised as she moved to sit up on the edge of the mattress.

"Thank you," she murmured.

But then, as if wary of accepting his help, she tugged her hand out of his clasp and avoided his eyes. On her own, she came to her feet and adjusted her clothes.

"Are you sure you're feeling okay?"

"I'm over the initial shock," she replied, "but that's all I'm sure of." She moved to the door. "If you're here when I come back, I'll see you then."

Rafe didn't say anything as she slipped out the door, because he wasn't certain he'd be there when she returned. *If* she returned.

Trusting anyone other than Lalie might be the biggest mistake he could make. One he couldn't afford.

4

TERRA GLANCED BACK at Rafe's luxury hideaway as she walked across the lawn with Lalie and Josh. She had a sense that Rafe was watching through the sheer curtains, although she couldn't see whether he was actually there behind them. *Rafe Jermain, Josh's father—alive!*

"You took a long time," Josh complained.

She strove to seem casual, as if the unthinkable hadn't happened. "Thank you for being patient while I was inside."

"Good boy," Lalie approved, tousling his hair. "Are you hungry for dinner and dessert, Josh?"

He nodded enthusiastically, then ran ahead of them, kicking his ball with renewed fervor.

Lalie stopped and touched Terra's arm. "What a shock for you."

"It was." Terra drew a deep breath, still feeling shaken and scattered. "I can't quite absorb it—or believe I fainted."

"You recognized Rafe right away?"

"Well, yes. I mean, after all the news about him five years ago, he was recognizable."

"Unfortunately so," Lalie lamented. "Terra, I'm so sorry. If I hadn't left the gate open, or if I hadn't given Josh a ball, this wouldn't have happened."

"You aren't responsible, Lalie. Really. My own curiosity is to blame. And I probably wouldn't have fainted if I hadn't skipped lunch on the plane."

Lalie sympathized, "Airline food doesn't have much appeal, I know." She walked slowly again toward the gate. "Maybe eating dinner will help settle you a little, even though it won't settle what you know now."

"I don't know what to think, Lalie."

"Well, I didn't either when Rafe showed up at my back door two months ago. It stopped my heart to see him, although I stayed on my feet somehow. He was half drowned, half dead from fever."

"Where had he been before that?"

"Montinerro. He was held prisoner, deep in the jungle there."

"But the news said he drowned after he was caught smuggling. They said sharks—" She couldn't go on.

Lalie nodded. "Rafe says it only looked as if he drowned. He got away, to Montinerro."

"All this time," Terra murmured, shaking her head, "he's been alive."

"Yes, all this time. And then a couple of months ago he escaped from the prison. He had a poor little raft— bamboo and inner tubes like the Cuban refugees came over on—and after he washed ashore he dragged himself home to Jermain's Island. Since then, I've nursed him halfway back to health, but he still has a ways to go."

"Does anyone else know about him?"

"Just us. Rafe doesn't want his family to know, and I agree with him." Lalie explained, "The Jermains have owned the hotel and half of the island since long before the Civil War. If there was a family conspiracy, and it ever came to light, it would take down a lot of people and the island economy, as well."

They reached the gate and passed through. Lalie closed and latched it, then paused, looking back at the estate. She turned imploring eyes on Terra.

"Rafe is innocent. I've known him since the day he was born. Never, *never* would he turn on this country."

Terra desperately wanted to believe Lalie's words. "It's hard to accept that he's alive, much less that he's innocent," she responded hesitantly.

"He'll explain what happened." Lalie gave another worried glance in his direction. "Unless he bolts and tries to hole up somewhere else. Whatever he thinks, he's not well enough to survive without help."

Josh came back to them at the gate right then, preventing any further conversation about Rafe.

Lalie took the boy's hand. "Let's get you washed up for dinner. I've made chicken corn chowder and popovers."

Terra followed them through the cozy kitchen to a hallway. She was still shaky within herself, her heart skipping beats over what she had discovered at the estate. Her mind still struggled to accept the fantastic fact that Rafe was next door, not dead, not devoured by sharks and maybe not guilty.

She couldn't yet begin to think of what that could mean for her and Josh, if it was true. She had never needed for something to be true as much as she needed it now.

But what if Lalie was wrong about Rafe? What if he wasn't innocent? What then?

Too confused to sort out her thoughts, she went on with Lalie and Josh to a bedroom where Lalie explained that Josh would nap when she baby-sat him in the future.

The boy was entranced when he saw that a free-standing canvas hammock stood in place of a bed. It had a colorful spread, pillows that matched and a collection of stuffed animals including Paddington Bear and Kermit the Frog. Delighted, Josh settled right into the hammock with the menagerie.

Leaving him there to play, Terra went with Lalie to the kitchen. Questions about Rafe were piling up in her mind.

"What is Rafe healing from?" she asked, while the older woman put the finishing touches to the corn chowder.

"Starvation, recurring fever, a sprained back, twisted knee." Lalie's lips tightened. "I hate to think what was done to him in that prison. He needs proper medical care, but can't risk having a doctor turn him in."

"No, I guess not," Terra reflected. "He only has you to depend on."

"And maybe you, now. Whatever good you can do him would help. Not that you shouldn't hear what he has to say first before you decide what you'll do."

Terra said, "I got the impression that he didn't plan to explain, that he'd be gone by the time I—" She stopped, abruptly aware of a silence in the nap room. "I'd better check on Josh."

She hastened to the bedroom and found him asleep, hugging Paddington to his cheek. He'd had a big, busy day, she thought, tucking the comforter around him. He needed rest right now, more than he needed dinner. She kissed his cheek and tiptoed out.

In the kitchen, she found Lalie hanging up the phone.

"I called Rafe," Lalie advised, "and he's still there, thank goodness. How is Josh doing?"

"He dropped off to sleep." Terra glanced at the phone. "Maybe I should go next door now instead of later."

Lalie agreed, taking up the phone again. "I'll call Rafe and tell him."

"How does he know it's you and not someone else?"

"Oh, we have a signal." Lalie explained that she let the estate phone ring three times first, then hung up and dialed again. Demonstrating, she dialed the second time and spoke to Rafe.

"Terra is coming over there now, okay? No, little Josh fell into a nap so I'm going to hold dinner awhile. Give her a snack to tide her over. Bye." She hung up, looking alarmed. "He sounded like he had one foot out the door already. Hurry, Terra."

Terra left her and rushed through the gate, down the long sloping lawn to the brick patio. She was breathless when she reached the French doors and knocked for Rafe to let her in.

For several moments there was no response. She tried the knob and found it locked. Then, slowly, it turned in her hand and the door opened.

"You move fast," Rafe said, motioning her in and locking the door after her. No longer bare chested, he was wearing a white T-shirt with the same snug denims she'd last seen him in.

"With Josh asleep, this seemed like a good time."

"You haven't had anything to eat yet, though."

"No, but I'm not hungry right now."

"Eat something, anyway."

"Really, I'm not—" She stopped as he clasped his hand around her wrist.

He gave a slight tug. "I don't want you fainting on me again. Come with me."

Terra didn't appreciate his peremptory manner, but the strong, warm pressure of his fingers was something else altogether, far more persuasion than command.

Knowing from her night with him what sensual passion his touch could generate in her, she didn't want to feel that way now. Still, she was feeling it, that same primal reaction she'd had to him five years earlier. Acute awareness. Erotic tension. Rising anticipation.

It didn't help that the palm of his hand seemed to be charged by a high-voltage current. Her skin felt a provocative shock from the contact.

He's guilty until he proves otherwise, Terra reminded herself. To forget it and feel attracted to him would be foolish and dangerous...unless he turned out to be truthful. She wasn't counting on miracles, yet she couldn't keep from holding out a trace of hope that her son's father was a good man, after all. It seemed impossible, though, despite his and Lalie's words to the contrary.

Terra stood her ground and drew her arm out of Rafe's hold. "All right, I'll have a bite of something."

"This way, then." He led her down a long hallway into a formal parlor. It was a grand old house, gracious and refined, furnished with international antiques and elegant artwork.

Terra noticed that Rafe limped badly as he walked. She recalled the injuries Lalie had enumerated.

"How did you hurt your leg?"

"A little of this, a little of that," he replied with a hard, bitter edge in his voice. "How did you miss lunch?"

"I didn't have an appetite then." She added emphatically, "Or now."

"Well, I don't have an appetite for picking you up off the floor a second time."

"Thank you for your help before, although you didn't need to bother. I could have recovered as well on the floor as on the bed."

"You're welcome, but not for implying that chivalry should be dead."

Increasingly annoyed with his curt remarks and obdurate attitude, she stopped in the middle of the parlor. "I hope your story is a short one, Mr. Jermain, because my offer to listen is wearing out fast."

"I'm not surprised, Ms. Camden." He gestured to a doorway. "The kitchen is through there."

She moved on ahead of him. "How do you know my full name?"

"Lalie briefed me about you and the baby-sitting." Despite his uneven gait, he caught up with her and took the lead again. "She said you're a menu specialist, not married and you live in San Francisco. Along with your name, that's all I know. It's nothing compared to what you know about me."

"I'd prefer to know nothing about you. You're obviously bad for my health."

"Terrific rapport we're building between us," he muttered gloomily.

He led her through a long dining room to the kitchen, where the seating area was a breakfast bar. She perched on the edge of a tall wicker chair he pulled out for her. Then he opened the fridge and took out a crock of cheese spread and a can of cola. He got crackers out of a cupboard, a knife from a drawer and set it all in front of her.

Terra took a sip of cola, aware of his eyes on her, watching every move. Maybe recognizing something familiar about her? No, he showed no hint of recognition.

To evade the unnerving effect of his scrutiny, she glanced around the large, beautifully outfitted kitchen. Long bay windows faced east, to an ocean view. Beyond them, a verdant lawn led down to a narrow beach. The water reflected the sunset and she could hear gentle surf breaking against the shore.

"This is quite a hiding place," she commented after her visual tour. "You've been here two months?"

"Back and forth between here and Lalie's. The owners don't know I'm a houseguest, much less alive. No one but Lalie knew until you walked in on me today."

He pulled out the seat next to hers and eased into it gingerly, favoring his back and the one leg. He was close enough for her to catch the shower-fresh scent of his skin, near enough that she could put a hand out and touch him without reaching very far.

She reached instead for a cracker, dabbed some spread on it and waited for him to say more. But he didn't elaborate any further. Silent and stone faced, he watched her lift the cracker to her lips. His attention was so piercing, so intense, that she set the cracker down uneaten.

"I'm just not hungry."

"You're also not going to believe anything I say."

She replied, "Your own skeptical attitude is making certain of that."

"It's been certain from the start."

"Only in your own mind."

"Like your mind is open."

"Yes."

"Why?"

Because of our son, she thought. *And because I owe you for saving my life that night.*

She replied, "Lalie's belief in you is one reason."

"One. Name another."

"My secretary would say it's because I'm a Libra with a Libran soft spot for the underdog. I'd say I'm simply fair-minded."

"Not in my case."

"I haven't heard your side of it yet, so how do you know?"

"Instinct. Mine tells me you live by the law, with all due respect for it."

"So does Lalie," she countered, "as far as I know."

"But she's my godmother, so her belief in me is emotional. You've never so much as gotten a parking ticket, I'll bet."

Already annoyed with him, Terra was irritated that much more by the condescending certainty in his tone and the fact that he was entirely accurate about her legal correctness.

"So what if I haven't?" she retorted. "It's not a major character flaw, and it doesn't mean I can't listen."

"Not with an open mind."

"Honestly, considering who you are, what do you expect? You broke an embargo, smuggled weapons to Montinerro and got caught red-handed. There were several eyewitnesses."

"The same witnesses swear I was done in by sharks. True or false?"

"You're alive," Terra conceded. "It's impossible, but true. Nonetheless, I don't believe that many witnesses lied. They were military personnel, sailors."

"I didn't say they lied. They only saw the surface. They—" He stopped and stared out the windows. "What's the use? I don't have to tell you what the press made of me. Like everyone else, you already know."

"Like everyone else, I presume the press had their facts straight. You supplied illegal arms to a brutal dictator."

"Not arms. Life-saving medicines. For the resistance army and the Montinerran people."

Terra scoffed, "That explains the cargo of guns and ammunition you were caught off-loading to the Montinerro navy."

"As a matter of fact, it does. And if I hadn't promised Lalie I'd tell you everything, I'd stop right there."

"A promise is a promise," Terra said. "How do you explain guns and ammunition?"

As if it was killing him to provide the details, he replied, "The ammo was filled with vaccine, not explosives. The weapons were a cover for the medical cargo, and my contact was a resistance operative who'd infiltrated the Montinerro military. He had a network for diverting my cargo to the freedom underground."

Terra would have given anything at that moment to wholly believe that he wasn't lying, wasn't a traitor, wasn't guilty. Yet she knew that prisons were full of guilty men who pleaded not guilty, and that courtrooms were full of honest eyewitnesses who sometimes mistook what they'd seen. She'd be naive not to suspect that Rafe was giving her the same line he'd give to a defense attorney.

"What you say sounds plausible, but if you were a good guy why did you jump ship?"

"Instinct, again. Something wasn't right that morning. I could feel it, but couldn't put a finger on it. Then a U.S. navy cutter showed up out of the blue, where no cutter should have been—not unless something was haywire. I sensed a setup and I was right."

"Who would set you up?"

Rafe's eyes hardened to ice. "My contact set me up. He turned traitor to the resistance, went over to the other side for profit and eliminated everybody he'd dealt with before. Now he's a Montinerran fat cat, a suck-up politico who skims major cream from trade profits with our country."

"Politico? What's his name?"

"It doesn't matter. What difference is there from one politician to the next, anyway? Especially in Montinerro."

"A name offers proof. No name offers none."

"Leon."

"Leon who?"

"Never mind, because I have plans for him. I don't want him tipped off to it by anyone. Next question."

Terra had plenty to ask. "Lalie says you were in prison, that you escaped."

"It was more like hell, and I escaped by the skin of my teeth."

He looked so bleak and anguished as he said it that she couldn't keep her heart from going out to him.

"Who put you there? Leon?"

"No, he needed me dead. The resistance canned me. I escaped to them, hoping I'd be welcomed as an ally. Surprise, surprise, whoever could vouch for me was dead. They only knew I was the American traitor who allegedly supplied their enemy. So they locked me in a dungeon and kept me as a secret bargaining chip."

"What exactly do you mean?"

"They hoped they'd get the upper hand on the regime one day. They knew my government would pay big to get its hands on me if it found out I was alive." He paused, jaw muscles ticking silently. "Covert operations are a tricky, cutthroat business."

"I know nothing about the shady side of life, I'm afraid," Terra said uncertainly.

"You know about me, which is already too much for your good and mine. Or your son's and Lalie's." He set his elbows on the counter and rubbed his fingers through his hair as if battling a migraine. "Innocent people. What a mess."

Terra thought of the consequences there would be if she did the right thing, if she turned Rafe in. She would be questioned, at the very least. Lalie would be arrested for harboring a criminal. As for Josh, Terra was horrified to think of him being questioned.

"Does Columbia know about you?"

"Doesn't have a clue. No one but Lalie, until now."

Terra recalled Lalie saying Rafe had internal bruises. Now they made sickening sense, if he'd been mistreated during his imprisonment. He looked half-starved, and dungeon pale.

Inching his fingers through his dark hair again, he said, "I shouldn't have come back here."

Terra asked herself if a guilty man would voluntarily come back to a country that loathed him. Or would only an innocent man return?

She touched his forearm and felt quivering tension in his tight, knotted muscles. She realized he was barely holding himself together, that his antagonistic rudeness might be his only defense mechanism.

"Rafe, there must be some way you could tell all this to the federal authorities and make them understand."

"Not with the feds and Montinerro in bed together now on diplomacy and trade. Not with Leon pulling strings in between. Either way, both countries want me dead. Coming back was insane. I shouldn't have thought I'd beat the risks. Risks I never calculated—like your little boy's blasted ball."

"Why *did* you come back?"

"I had a plan to prove myself, until you came along. All I needed was time, a few more weeks."

"A plan," she repeated.

He gave a defeated sighed. "It might even have worked."

Thinking of Josh, and also of the debt she owed her son's father, Terra took a deep breath. "Rafe . . ."

"What?"

She plunged off the deep end. "For the time being, I give you the benefit of the doubt."

"Sure you do."

"I'm serious."

"You can't be." He lowered his hands and shook his head in disbelief. "You're a mother with a boy to think of. And yourself, as well."

She argued, "I'll keep your secret. Believe me."

"But why would you—" Rafe broke off, looking floored. "I mean, you've got nothing to gain and too much to lose."

Terra shrugged. "I'm a Libra. You're an underdog. And Lalie's belief in you goes a long way with me."

"Forget it, Terra." His gruff, off-putting tone was back. "Bringing you into this is going too far."

"I'm already in, Rafe. You have no choice."

"I can still shove off on my own. With me gone, no-body's at risk."

"What about you?" Terra said. "The shape you're in, you won't get far."

"It's a risk I'll have to take."

Terra wasn't about to surrender the slim hope she now had, the only hope Josh would ever have. She turned in her chair and laid a guilt trip on Rafe.

"If you shove off, you'll break Lalie's heart."

Rafe muttered a curse. He pushed away from the bar, limped to the windows and stared out for several minutes. Finally, he turned and threw up his hands.

"So I'll stick around," he growled. "For the time being."

RAFE STOOD INSIDE, behind the curtains, and watched Terra walk from the estate to Lalie's. Through the curtain sheers, his eyes followed her across the brick patio to the sweeping green lawn and up the long slope. The evening breeze played through her hair and rippled the back of her white sleeveless blouse.

God, he'd love to be that breeze right then. It had all the freedom in the world to touch her lips . . . caress the smooth skin of her slim, graceful legs...swirl upon her ripe, full breasts.

Years without a woman, and just his luck it wasn't the Wicked Witch of the West who walked in on him. No, it was delectable, desirable Terra Camden, and she'd left him with a hungry heart to add to his bum knee, wrenched back, bruised insides and periodic fevers.

Given those other miseries, he shouldn't be making it twice as hard on himself by watching her return to Lalie's house. He'd rather think it was just his sex drive kicking up a fuss over her, but it was more. She had an unwelcome, unexplainable effect on his emotions, enough to make him want to forget she was the most dangerous woman he'd ever met.

Something about her seemed familiar, something he couldn't pin down. Oddly, he was sure he knew just how it would feel to kiss her. He didn't wonder how it would feel, he simply knew.

Under less threatening circumstances, he would have been excited by what he was feeling for her. Until Terra walked in, he'd been sure his sexual function was a casualty of his prison experience. Correction: hellhole, not prison, was the word for that putrid hovel of horror.

Still, wonder of wonders, he had a surge of sexual energy. The response didn't overjoy him as it would have if Terra Camden weren't the stimulus.

Instead of lusting for her, he should be mistrusting her. What guarantee did he have that she really meant to give him the benefit of the doubt? Even if she meant it now, she could change her mind a minute later.

He couldn't afford to forget that one phone call from her to the law would guarantee a quick, no-questions-asked end of his life courtesy of Leon.

Despite all that, he couldn't unglue his eyes from their view of Terra. Couldn't stop mentally taking her in his arms and kissing her senseless. Too easily, he could picture himself making love to her. He'd have a hell of a time sleeping tonight if this kept up.

His breath caught as he saw Terra pause at the top of the slope. She turned and looked in his direction. He knew she couldn't see him from that distance, not through the sheers, yet he almost apologized out loud for his imagination.

Although certain he couldn't be seen, he stepped back a little from the doors. She stood very still where she was, seeming to stare straight into his soul, then pivoted and went through the picket gate.

Rafe thought more seriously than ever about clearing out. If it wasn't for Lalie, he'd be gone already. Hell, if he had been ruthless enough about staying alive, he would have left Terra Camden unconscious on the bathroom floor and made a run for it then. He wouldn't have called Lalie for help.

He wouldn't still be here, torn in two about what Terra should or shouldn't do, would or wouldn't do. He hardly knew her, yet he was letting her make him irrational. What if she'd been bluffing, playing for time to get to a phone so she could report him and Lalie? He'd be smartest to make his move now instead of trusting a stranger.

The more he thought about it, the closer he leaned toward getting out while he could, even if it meant breaking Lalie's heart. Not to mention never seeing Terra Camden again.

5

LALIE WAS SEATED at the kitchen table, looking apprehensive, when Terra returned from the estate. Terra sat down with her.

"Josh is still napping," Lalie said. "How did it go with Rafe?"

"He explained, but he's suspicious of me. Very mistrustful."

"What do you think now that you've heard him out?"

"I'd like to believe what he says, although I don't know him as well as you do."

"He convinced you, then. At least a little."

"I'm willing to reserve judgment at this point," Terra said. "He mentioned a plan to prove himself, but he didn't give any details."

"He won't talk about it any more than to say he's got one, Terra. The less I know, the better, he says. I do know I'm not the only American with a wholehearted belief in him, although it may seem that way to you from all the news you heard."

"It seems possible that the headlines were wrong."

"Bless you," Lalie said, bowing her head. "When I first set eyes on you in San Francisco, my special angel told me you were a young lady with a big heart. You still are."

Terra demurred, "I don't know about that. Simply fair-minded is more like it. At any rate, Rafe and I came to a temporary understanding that I'll keep the secret and he'll stay put."

"The question is," Lalie said worriedly, "how long?"

"That's up to Rafe. He says he hates endangering us."

Lalie nodded. "I'm a conspirator, no regrets about it for myself. But then, my child is an adult who will understand if I ever go to prison for this. Your little Josh will be without you if it's ever discovered what you know about Rafe."

Terra was silent, agonizing, then she said, "Lalie, if I told you my deepest secret, would you keep it, no matter what?"

"Of course. Just as I've kept Rafe a secret, I'd keep yours. Whatever it is."

"It has to do with Rafe. He's . . ."

"Terra, what?"

In a painful whisper, Terra revealed, "Josh is Rafe's son."

Lalie went completely still, staring at her with wide, unblinking eyes. "His . . . ?"

"Son," Terra repeated softly. "No one else knows."

Lalie's eyes went closed and she shook her head slightly as if comprehending was a struggle. For some time she stayed that way, then her eyelids fluttered open. "Rafe . . . and you? How?"

Terra gave a helpless nod and haltingly began to explain.

BY THE TIME she finished, both she and Lalie were clasping hands on the tabletop, all choked up.

"Oh, my heavenly Lord," Lalie murmured. "So that's how you got Josh."

"I'm afraid so."

"You aren't sorry to have him."

"No, never. I've only been sorry that Rafe was the man."

"Terra, he didn't seem to recognize you at all."

Terra shrugged. "I had long hair that night, bleached blond for spring break. Looking in the mirror then, I hardly recognized myself, and even my girlfriends were amazed at how different blond hair made me look."

"Do you intend to keep Rafe in the dark about this?"

"I don't know. I need time to think it through and weigh what to do. If Rafe turns out to be innocent, maybe I'd want him to know. If he's guilty, though . . ."

"I see what you mean," Lalie said, looking torn. "For as long as you want, your secret is safe with me." Her face creased in a sad smile. "I know life isn't all moonlight and roses and happy endings the way everyone would like it to be."

"No, not for me."

"Terra, you've done your best in your own set of circumstances, and that's something for you to be proud of. Your good mothering and your family's support shows in your son."

"It's so hard sometimes, Lalie. I doubt myself so often, worry that I'm not spending enough time with Josh. Or that other single mothers are so much better at it than I am."

Terra was grateful to unburden herself a little more. Lalie's innate kindness, soothing touch and receptive warmth just brought it all tumbling out.

"Of course it's hard," Lalie agreed. "With no serious challenges and hardships to face, how else would we learn, how would we grow into better people? You're smarter and better for your struggles, from what I see, and I'll bet Josh is, too."

Terra gave her a grateful smile. "You're improving my perspective on myself."

"Good. Now, how about us having some dinner for ourselves?"

They served up the chowder and popovers, then settled down again to eat. While Lalie said grace, Terra thought, *I'm in this up to my ears now.*

From now on, she was committed to constant anxiety, desperate hope and gnawing doubt. Whatever happened after this was anyone's guess.

Was she conspiring to hide a criminal? Or was she giving an unjustly incriminated man a fair break? Would she ever really know?

Josh appeared in the kitchen doorway, rubbing the sleep out of his eyes, and Terra motioned him to sit in her lap and wake up.

"I see it now," Lalie murmured. "The blue eyes and the same chin. It's there, now that I know."

Unaware, Josh snuggled against Terra and yawned. Terra held him close, asking herself if she was doing the right thing by conspiring with Rafe.

In so many ways she was still in a daze. Too much was happening, far more than she had ever feared or anticipated even in her wildest imagination. Her thoughts veered between faint hope and stark terror.

She questioned, *Do you know what you're doing? Are you insane or what?*

There was no saying, not with any degree of certainty. Discovering Rafe had shaken her world and displaced its axis. Terra couldn't even imagine what knots she'd be in if the invitation to dinner with Rafe's grandparents had been tonight instead of tomorrow.

But, all things considered, would tomorrow night be any easier to handle? She wasn't counting on anything after this, except that *anything* could and might happen.

THE NEXT MORNING BROUGHT sunlight and a phone call to Terra's room. She didn't need either one to wake her up after having a mostly sleepless night plagued by doubts about her sanity, Rafe himself and the dangerous decision she'd made to keep him a secret.

"Morning," Columbia greeted on the other end. "Good news. I've got my sous chef back. How does nine-thirty to eleven sound for our first meeting tomorrow?"

"Fine," Terra agreed. "What about afternoon?"

"I'm not sure yet. In the meantime, get acquainted with the business center for secretarial services. Elise Jennings manages it."

"Good idea, I'll do that."

"What did you and mama arrange for Josh?"

"I'll take him there each morning, spend lunchtime with him, then collect him around four every afternoon."

"Great. See you nine-thirty, tomorrow. The concierge or any of the bellmen can direct you to my office. By the way, don't forget to enjoy the vacation part of your time here, or I'll feel guilty."

"Enjoyment is a given at a place like this," Terra assured her, even though relaxation wasn't an option after her earth-shaking discovery yesterday. Rafe's existence was definitely not a stress-buster.

Terra hung up the phone and turned her attention to Josh, who was getting out of the trundle bed. He crawled in under her covers to cuddle.

She kissed him good-morning. "How's my little dreamer?"

He gave a big yawn and silently continued waking up. Terra glanced at the empty side of the bed as she sifted her fingers through his silky dark hair. An image came to her of Rafe lying there, of the three of them snuggling together—a family affair.

Then another image formed, one from memory, of herself and Rafe in his sailboat, entwined with each other, locked in passion, shuddering with pleasure.

And making a baby, in spite of the protection they'd used. Rafe had saved her life that night; together, they'd unknowingly brought another life into being.

For the rest of her life and even beyond it, she was linked indelibly to Rafe Jermain. Because of him, she was alive today. Alive, well and mother to their child.

Not their love child, for they hadn't been in love. Josh, to her sad regret, was passion's child, a passion she hadn't known until Rafe lit her fire. Still, there had been sweetness and romance in their passion, so fervently imaginative and exuberant, never cheap or tawdry.

Rafe had taken great care with her. Exquisite care. She had known even then that she'd never have another lover like him. She had dated a few men since then—fewer of them more than halfheartedly—and learned from being intimate a couple of times how right she'd been about Rafe.

He'd been simply, without a doubt, the best there could be.

Maybe he still was, she mused painfully. But what of it, in that case? Finding out either way wasn't the reason she was giving him the benefit of the doubt now. Yet, a small inner voice said her reasons didn't actually exclude a precipitating urge to find out.

Her purpose was to discover the truth about his guilt or innocence, not about his sexual charm. So she should be reminding herself all along that he had once been so virile that a condom hadn't contained him. She wouldn't risk anything romantic with him again, would she?

Ridiculous even to be arguing about it with herself night and day. Time and again. Never reaching a proper conclusion....

ON THE WAY THROUGH the lobby to breakfast in the dining room, Terra stopped at the concierge desk and got acquainted with Joanie Griffin. Friendly and up-beat, with a can-do attitude, Joanie was in her late twenties, recently married to Steve Lantz.

"Once you get started at work," Joanie said, "you'll want to be in touch with Elise Jennings who runs the business center. Whatever business machines and sec-retarial service you need, she's the resource."

Terra nodded. "Columbia mentioned the center."

"She says you're really a whiz, Terra."

Terra grinned. "She said the same about you."

"Well, are we flattered no end, or what?"

Terra laughed with her, enjoying the immediate rapport. She noticed the sparkling diamond ring Joanie wore on the ring finger of her left hand.

"It's beautiful, Joanie."

Joanie's laughter softened and her eyes glowed. "Thanks. I love it with all my heart. I'm married to Steve, the marketing manager here." She glanced down at Josh. "Now that I'm a wife, I'm looking forward to motherhood. Your son is a living doll."

Then, getting down to business, Joanie efficiently arranged the use of a golf cart for Terra to go back and forth to Lalie's. Carts and special minivans were the main form of island transportation for the resort's guests and employees.

Joanie called for the cart to be brought to the front door so Terra could go exploring after breakfast. Setting down the phone, she glanced across the lobby.

"Oh, there's Liz, the general manager. Have you met? No?"

She signaled to Liz Jermain, who came over to them, and introduced Terra. Liz was thirtysomething, a beauty with glossy brown shoulder-length hair. She wore a chic, colorful, silk suit and had an air of independence about her. Terra already knew that Liz was Rafe's only sister, but she hadn't known she was blue-eyed, like him.

Giving a gracious smile, Liz shook Terra's hands. "We're so glad you could come, Terra." She bent down to Josh and shook his hand, too. "Young Josh, how are you?"

"My ears went pop in the airplane," he replied.

Terra went perfectly still as Liz bent a little lower, looking into his face. Liz glanced up at her and then back to Josh with increasing, unwavering intensity.

Terra told herself it was unlikely that Liz would make any connection between Josh and Rafe. After all, Lalie hadn't perceived it until she learned the facts.

"My golly, Josh," Liz said, "what utterly blue eyes you have."

He nodded. "Like Grando."

Terra felt a surge of relief and silently blessed Josh for his matter-of-fact, all-in-the-family reply. Thank heaven that her father's eyes, pale bluish gray, had at least a smidgen of color in common with Josh's. It was slight, but it was there, and Andrew often made a proud point of it.

"Remarkable," Liz said, straightening up. "Blue runs in my family, as well."

"Mine, too," Joanie put in.

"And bluebirds," said Josh.

Liz rumpled his hair and laughed. "Definitely. What a cutie you are."

Right then, her pager sounded. She apologized for the interruption, excused herself and returned to her office. Then Joanie's phone rang. Terra pushed off from the desk, waved goodbye and continued with Josh to the main dining room.

It was elegant, almost too much so for the morning meal, yet an appropriate way to start the first full day at a posh resort. As soon as they were seated, Terra started taking notes about the room—the decor, lighting, seating capacity, atmosphere, degree of formality and so forth.

Eventually, she would do the same for every one of the resort's dining areas, including the banquet rooms. She planned to take snapshots of each area from various angles for the graphic designer who would need to adapt the menu to the physical design of the dining area.

Working as a menu specialist involved more than word-crafting the menu, although that aspect was highly important, even crucial. It was a vital part of Terra's business to know that even the best wording couldn't shine without a perfect format, which included the proper choice of paper, color, type style, binding.

There were decisions to make about whether the menu would be one page or many pages. How many vertical folds there would be, if any. Where each menu item would be placed on the format. How related items would be grouped.

Would the paper be lightweight, heavy, perhaps laminated? How would the prices be shown? Would the descriptions be flowery, lively or straightforward? Would everything be centered, or some items off-center?

If she hadn't had Aunt Claire as her mentor, Terra would have still been learning the fine points of her work. Thanks to Claire, though, and a natural affinity for words, she knew she had more going for her than the average menu specialist.

The best thing about it right now was that it kept Terra's mind off Rafe. But that didn't last long.

"Mommy, are you working?" Josh asked, watching her pencil skim over her notepad.

"You bet I am. Just like at home and in my own office."

He glanced around at the other diners. "Is my daddy at work?"

"Maybe." She quickly changed the subject. "Finished with your cereal? Great. Ready to explore the island a little?"

He gave an enthusiastic nod and she hustled him outside to get his mind off the daddy question. They found the cart at the front door, waiting for them. Shad Teach was there as well, his wily blue eyes seeming to spark with mischief, his golden earring glinting in the sunlight. He showed Terra the basics of operating the cart, then helped her into it with a courtly flourish.

Settling Josh in beside her, he asked, "Off to where, today?"

"Lalie's house," Josh replied, looking as thrilled as if the destination were Disneyland.

Terra corrected him, "No, that's tomorrow, Monday. Today is Sunday."

Josh's mouth turned down and Shad chuckled. "Everybody loves Lalie Hanes," he said. "A gift to the human community she is. Fine, fine woman."

Terra recalled Columbia's comment that Shad knew everyone and everything. He certainly knew how upstanding Lalie was. Did he know *all* about her? Terra wondered. Was it true that no one else knew of Rafe's presence? Perhaps Shad? Maybe Liz? Possibly Columbia even, though Rafe had denied it?

She saw Shad's eyes fixing on Josh's features. Again, she tensed inside.

"That's quite a pair of baby-blues you look at the world with, lad."

Apparently in reaction to the word *baby*, Josh gave an indignant reply. "I'm four and a half." He held up the correct number of fingers, including the half, to illustrate.

"Oh, yes, indeed," Shad affirmed hastily, looking quite sheepish about offending Josh's pride.

Eager to leave, Terra offered a quick thanks for his help and drove away. Any more tense moments and she'd be a nervous wreck.

AFTER LEISURELY EXPLORING the village and the island all day, Terra returned to the hotel late in the afternoon. While out and about she had relaxed somewhat, but the prospect of an evening with Miz Elizabeth and Judge Cameron tied her nerves in knots as the time approached.

"You must be a very good boy tonight," Terra reminded Josh that evening when they got ready for dinner. "No slurping your soup. No milk mustaches. No forgetting the four magic words."

Josh grimaced and recited them. "Please, thanks, ma'am, sir."

"Excellent."

Dressed in a crisp, white-and-navy sailor suit, he looked quite the little gentleman. Terra wasn't keen on the naval style of the suit, but it was a gift to Josh from her parents, so she'd dutifully packed it along on the trip. Josh insisted on wearing it tonight.

Besides, Miz Elizabeth and Judge Bradshaw would probably be as charmed by Josh's outfit as her parents were. Maybe it would distract them from the family traits Josh inherited. Or maybe their reaction to his features would be the same as Liz's had been—a moment of intent scrutiny followed by a marveling shake of the head.

Terra powder-blushed her cheeks and ran a comb through her hair. In the mirror, she checked out the image she projected in her taupe silk dress. None of her discomposure showed; there was no outward evidence that she'd stumbled upon Rafe Jermain yesterday. Looking at her, no one would ever suspect that her life had turned wrong side up since she'd arrived in Bride's Bay.

She searched for and found no visible sign of her gnawing fear that Rafe's grandmother would set eyes on Josh and know at once that he was Rafe's offspring.

"You look pretty, ma'am," Josh offered impishly.

Terra curtsied and put on a confident smile for him. "Thank you, sir. Ready to go?"

Hand in hand they left their room and went to the far end of the west wing. Judge Bradshaw answered the door. Terra guessed that he was in his late seventies or early eighties. A portly, handsome gentleman, he had a wild shock of gray hair that topped a weathered, grandfatherly face. His voice, inflected by a slow Southern drawl, was quiet and kindly.

"Good evening, come in." He shook hands with them both. "We're very pleased that you could join us tonight."

After seating them in a lovely parlor furnished with antiques from the Old South's glory days, he advised, "Elizabeth is taking a tedious phone call from the security chief." He clucked his tongue. "Security weighs heavily on everyone's minds these days, I'm afraid. She'll be with us shortly."

He ambled around in a charming, absentminded fashion, getting a glass of wine for Terra and apple juice for Josh. Glancing around the room, Terra was startled to see a framed photo of Rafe amid several other pictures grouped on top of a console table. She hastily covered her reaction so the judge wouldn't notice.

But he caught it, even though he was busy handing Josh the juice at that moment.

"Blood runs as thick as winter molasses in my wife's family," he remarked pointedly, sitting down across from her with his own drink. "Once a Jermain, always a Jermain."

"Of course," Terra politely agreed, as if notorious traitors were common features in everyone's pictorial history.

"A sad chapter in the family history, though," he went on. "As far as we're concerned, Rafe is innocent. Your own opinion may differ, which is understandable, considering how much bad news there was about him."

Terra acknowledged, "I followed the story at the time. I mean, the newspaper headlines and TV reports were hard to avoid." She added, "Also, my parents are in the military, so it was a topic of discussion."

His face creased in a benign smile. "Army officers, aren't they?"

"Yes, chaplains, but how do you know that?"

"I'm not sure." He looked puzzled at himself. "Picked it up somewhere, I suppose, from Columbia or someone . . ." He trailed off and then waved a hand absently. "Elizabeth will remember for me."

His blue-gray eyes lit as a willowy, silver-haired woman of his own age entered the room. She wore a simple but elegant knit dress of a vivid blue that matched her eyes. Her gracious smile, erect posture and quick, determined stride marked her unmistakably as the grande dame of the Jermain family.

Terra stood, heart in her throat, and tugged Josh to his feet. She shook the firm, slender hand Elizabeth Jermain offered to her.

"Forgive me," Rafe's grandmother implored, "for letting hotel business deprive me of greeting you properly."

Terra made nothing of it. "As a business owner myself, I completely understand."

"Me, too," Josh piped up stoutly. "Ma'am."

The older woman's gaze settled on him with the same sudden absorption her granddaughter had shown earlier. "A cutie," she observed, "just as Liz described you."

She went silent for a long moment, studying him, then shook her shoulders lightly as if dismissing a thought and sat down next to Cameron.

"What long-winded tale was my husband enthralling you with in my absence?" She patted the judge's hand lovingly.

"A mystery, my dear," he said. "Can you remember where I picked up the idea that Ms. Camden's family has a military background?"

"I'm afraid I can, and I regret to say it has more to do with strict security policy than I'd like." She gave Terra an apologetic look. "No one comes here to work without a thorough background check being done on them by our Thomas Graves. Since I own the resort, he keeps us informed, and yours is the most recent brief we've had."

"I'm not all that surprised, then," Terra said, feeling doubly on edge, although it was no fault of theirs. "I understand that the resort often hosts sensitive political meetings and conferences."

Elizabeth nodded. "Yes, there's a conference of diplomats coming up soon, in fact. Not a state secret by any means but still a security-intensive event. No doubt you've read rumors that the President and First Lady might vacation here next month."

Terra confirmed that she'd heard about it.

"A presidential visit would be an honor for us," Elizabeth said, "but no official word has gone out yet from the White House. He may be here, and also may not, as press rumors go."

The judge sighed, obviously discomfited by his social blunder. "I am chagrined that I mentioned anything at all from your background file. Senility must be creeping up on my manners."

Elizabeth patted his hand again and deftly turned the subject to a conversational advantage. "Terra, your work sounded so interesting that we wanted to know more about it from you, personally. And we were also delighted to learn you would bring Josh with you. So few children are guests here and they're always a treat."

Terra felt certain that the slurpy, gargly sounds Josh was making with his juice weren't what Elizabeth was referring to, but the older couple didn't act bothered by it. Of course, maybe that had more to do with Southern hospitality than indulgent indifference.

She nudged him with her elbow. "Josh. Manners, please."

Instead of obeying, he gulped down a mouthful with a vibrating *gunnggg* sound.

Terra warned, "No dessert if this keeps up."

He kept at it, as if misbehaving and mortifying his mother had suddenly become his life's goal. Then, suddenly, he set down his glass, scooted off the couch and ran to the picture of Rafe.

Pointing at it, he announced, "That's me when I get big."

Terra was floored, nearly speechless. She sputtered a command for him to come back and sit down. But Miz Elizabeth stood and went to him.

"There is a certain similarity," she murmured, moving Josh side by side with the portrait. "Don't you think so, Cameron?"

The judge cocked his head, nodding somewhat uncertainly. "Perhaps." He glanced at Terra. "What do you think?"

"Oddly enough," she managed to reply. "Yes. I sort of see what Josh means." She gave her son a motherly frown. "Take your seat again, please."

"What I see most clearly," the judge observed with an indulgent smile, "is that Josh needs more than grownup conversation to interest him."

He stood and took charge of the boy. "Come with me to my study and let's find ourselves a deck of cards. Excuse us, ladies."

Terra murmured an apology to Elizabeth after they left. "He's been so well-behaved until now."

"Think nothing of it, Terra." Elizabeth touched the portrait of Rafe. "My grandson here used to be the same way when he was that age. Strange they look rather alike."

Terra groped for words and came up with a monumental lie. "Especially strange since there's no relation on either side."

"Of course not." Elizabeth returned and sat down looking apologetic. "If I've offended you by comparing Joshua favorably to Rafe, I'm sorry, Terra. Few people share my belief that my grandson was not what everyone thinks he was, rest his soul."

Terra wished she could open her heart to Elizabeth and reveal that Rafe wasn't dead. The poor lady had tears in her eyes—loving, mournful tears. What joy it would give her to know that her grandson had survived.

But all Terra could do was reassure her, "Oh, I'm not offended. I'm pretty much neutral on the issue, actually."

"Well, then, let's leave it behind." Elizabeth blinked her tears away. "Tell me how you go about being a menu specialist."

Relieved to be off the subject of Rafe, Terra surmised that Columbia had probably briefed Elizabeth to some extent already. And the security check must have filled in the rest. She had to accept that it probably revealed Josh's birth record: father unknown.

What would Elizabeth say if she knew Rafe was Josh's father? That Rafe was on Jermain's Island, alive?

"It's creative work for the most part," Terra replied to Elizabeth's request. "Often unusual, and usually a challenge."

To illustrate, she described the rutabaga problem she and Macy had brainstormed for the Americana project.

Elizabeth laughed. "I must remember that the next time I'm served beets or parsnips. They'll go down far more easily as Heritage Vegetables."

They went on chatting about the hotel and restaurant business. It became clear that Elizabeth had no hobbies; her sole concern was the business of owning the resort.

"Liz," she said, "is the only one of my grandchildren interested in Bride's Bay Resort. Thank goodness for her, since it would break my heart to sell this place. So much family history here, you know, the roots run deep. Liz carries on and runs most everything in the family tradition, bless her."

Cameron came back into the room with Josh. They seated themselves at a bridge table in the corner and proceeded to enjoy an exuberant game of slapjack.

Elizabeth cheered them on periodically while maintaining a cordial conversation with Terra about the importance of family values and traditions in a child's life.

At just the right time, when the game score stood in Josh's favor, a maid opened the double doors to the dining room and announced that dinner was ready.

They had boneless quail, Madeira gravy, herbed grits and squash blossom salad. Dessert was a butter torte, multilayered with grape preserves, which gave Terra a brainstorm the moment it was served.

She asked Elizabeth, "How does Scuppernong Jam Cake strike you as a menu name for this?"

"Brilliant! No wonder you've earned such high marks in your specialty."

Terra grinned, not overly proud of herself, but very pleased to hear that she had earned an A + from Miz Elizabeth Jermain. That was the main reason she'd been invited, of course, to pass muster with the grande dame of Bride's Bay Resort.

Scuppernong. Piece of cake. With that, she knew Camden Consulting had officially arrived in South Carolina. Columbia would love the cake name, too. So Southern, so traditional, just right.

Things didn't continue so smoothly, however. Josh's restless spirit reared its head again and almost spilled his milk.

Terra saw that lingering over coffee would be courting trouble. "Would you mind very much if Josh and I call it a night?"

"Not at all," said Elizabeth with warm understanding. "He did wonderfully well tonight. When I was Josh's age, I couldn't sit still more than two minutes."

"Still can't," the judge teased her.

Terra left smiling, yet with deeply felt regrets that Josh couldn't have a family relationship to them, and neither could she.

Walking down the hall, she swung his hand. "They're nice people, aren't they?"

"Yep. Like Grando and Granda."

Terra felt so proud of him, and yet so terribly torn about his identity. For five years Josh's father had been her deep, dark secret. Now he was that much more of one. And now she had one more secret: she was afraid that she was as infatuated with him as she'd been the first time.

6

AFTER BREAKFAST Monday morning, Terra took Josh to Lalie's house for his first stay there. He bounded out of the golf cart and ran ahead of her to knock on the door.

Lalie came around the corner of the house. "There you are," she said. "Right on time. Come in back with me and I'll show you what you missed seeing on Saturday."

They followed her to the garden plots and greenhouses where she grew specialty produce for Columbia's kitchen and the resort.

"I've got baby romaine and Swift's lettuce leafing out so nicely right now, and lots of herbs, bouquet flowers, orchids . . ."

She led them on an interesting, absorbing tour of the greenhouses and vegetable patches. The orchids, especially, were an earthly delight. Lalie explained that not all of the exotic plants were hers; she was orchid-sitting many of them for estate owners who lived only part-time on the island.

At the end of the tour, she put Josh to work pulling weeds, then drew Terra aside for a private word.

"Rafe has to stay here with me today," she said.

Terra gulped and glanced at the house. "Here? Why?"

"Because every Monday morning the house cleaners go in next door. The gardeners mow the lawn today, too. Terra, I'm not sure Rafe can stay hidden from Josh all day. I can't keep an eye on everything every minute, you know?"

Terra let the fact sink in. She hadn't fully realized until now how complicated it was to hide Rafe, how much forethought, timing and careful planning it took. One little slip—such as the open gate the other day—and he'd be exposed.

"Would you mind if they met?"

"Lalie, if they did Josh might mention him to someone."

"True, but if Josh doesn't know Rafe by his real name, it wouldn't give him away."

"What does Rafe think about it?"

"We mulled it over and he figures no one will think anything if Josh mentions someone named Kermit at my house."

Terra recalled one of the stuffed animals on the hammock. "As in Kermit the Frog," she surmised.

"We only have today and next Monday to worry about it," Lalie said.

"I don't know, Lalie. Involving Josh in any way seems awfully irresponsible."

"He isn't all yours, Terra. He's Rafe's child, too, and maybe they should know each other on some level at least. Rafe is so lonely, trying not to go stir-crazy while his body and his spirit are healing."

Terra bit down on her lower lip to stem a tide of emotion. "Maybe you're right."

"He's in the kitchen at the moment, waiting for me to let him know one way or the other."

Terra agonized a moment more, then called to Josh. "Let's go inside, sweetheart. Lalie has somebody she wants us to meet."

Josh came running, hands dirty from uprooting weeds. "Who?"

Rafe was at the table, lifting a coffee cup to his mouth, when they came in. He pushed back in his chair and stood, giving Terra a wary look. Then he switched his focus to Josh.

Seeing Rafe's eyes widen, Terra held her breath. But after seeming surprised and baffled by what he saw, he gave a slight smile and introduced himself.

"Hi, I'm Kermit."

Josh looked up at him. "Really?"

"Yep, really Kermit. I hear your name is Josh."

"Yeah." Josh looked up at Terra. "This is Mommy."

Rafe put a hand out to Terra as if they were meeting for the first time. "Ma'am. How are you today?"

"Fine, thank you." Terra managed a nervous smile and experienced a surge of warmth when she shook his hand. He clasped hers a little longer than necessary and then slowly released it.

Josh tugged on her other hand. "I gotta go, Mom."

"Right this way," Lalie said, whisking him out of the kitchen.

Knees weak, Terra stood looking at Rafe across the table. "Kermit," she said, at a loss for anything else to say.

His lips quirked. "Nice boy you've got. Reminds me a lot of me when I was a kid."

Terra had been afraid of that, but she did all she could not to show it. "If you ran your mother ragged," she said lightly, "you're right."

"I did my best," he confirmed, pulling out a chair for her. "Have a seat if you feel like it."

Terra wasn't sure how she felt. She wasn't really prepared to see Rafe, and it put her off balance. Out of the blue she had an image of the way she'd first seen him yesterday—stark naked, steamy clean, all man. The thought sent her blood rushing to her cheeks.

"Okay, don't," he said gruffly, making it clear that her hesitation had a chilling effect on him. He sat down again and took a drink of his coffee, eyes narrowed on her over the rim of the cup.

She regretted that they'd gotten off on the wrong foot with each other again, yet she couldn't explain that she felt too vulnerable about the situation, too uncertain about his innocence or guilt and much too attracted to him.

"I have to leave in a minute," she told him, but then reluctantly took the seat he had offered.

Rafe observed dryly, "You haven't changed your mind about turning me in, I guess."

"Obviously not, since I haven't turned you in," Terra replied, matching his cool, sardonic tone.

He drummed his fingers on the table. "Not yet, you haven't."

Terra met his eyes. They were a brilliant, edgy blue. He had a white T-shirt on, faded jeans and sneakers. In spite of being thin, pale and rife with suspicion, he looked so good, so purely male, so very much Josh's father. And so sexy it made her heart race.

"We have an understanding," she said. "Remember?"

"Sure I do. I lost a few memories in prison, but nothing recent."

"You suspect my motives?"

"You know I do."

"As I said, the bottom line is I haven't turned you in, Kermit."

"I keep expecting you to."

"Why?"

"Because I don't have much faith left in human nature. Prison took it out of me."

"Before that, were you as much of a cynic as you seem to be now?"

"No, I was a good guy before I learned how easily they get shot down. But you're pretty sure I was never a good guy in the first place, aren't you?"

"I'm willing to wait for proof that you're as good as Lalie says. In the meantime, you seem sincere."

"You seem sincere, too, Terra. Which keeps me nervous about you."

"Rafe, are you goading me with your doubts so that I *will* have you arrested?"

"No. I'm just not sure I can trust you."

Lalie came back to the kitchen right then and caught them glaring at each other. "This is no time to be scrapping," she scolded. "United we stand, but dividing isn't going to get anybody's innocence proven."

Rafe withdrew into testy, disgruntled silence as Lalie set a photo album on the table in front of Terra.

"Look through this," she said, "while I take Josh outside with me."

Josh came skipping into the kitchen and Lalie sent him out ahead of her. At the back door she paused and gave Rafe a stern look. "You be nice or I'll turn you in myself."

Opening the album cover, Terra found that the first photo was portrait-sized. It showed Lalie, at a much younger age, holding a baby in a christening blanket.

Terra looked up at Rafe again. "You?"

He gave a curt nod and looked away. Far away.

Terra continued through the album, a visual history of Rafe's life: his first tooth, first Eagle Scout badge, first scholarship award, first fish caught with a fly reel. As well, he was pictured with family and friends at various events: school graduations, holidays, church functions, sailing regattas.

One snapshot showed him in an Independence Day parade, marching in a color guard, carrying the Stars and Stripes. Another had him receiving a good-citizen's award in high school.

In each image of Rafe, Terra noted a resemblance to Josh. But if Rafe had noticed the same thing, he wasn't saying.

The final photo showed him as Terra remembered him years earlier, on the deck of his sailboat. He had the wind in his dark hair and the gleam of adventure in his blue eyes. She slowly closed the album. Looking up, she found Rafe studying her.

"You remind me of someone," he mused, "but who?"

She shrugged as if she couldn't imagine reminding him of anyone. "I don't know."

"Or maybe we've met before."

"I don't see how," Terra said, shaking her head to convey that he was talking nonsense.

He sat back in his chair, undeterred by her response. "Something about you. I can't quite get a handle on it, though."

Lalie came back in, distracting him. She touched the photo album and asked Terra, "Does that look to you like a life gone wrong?"

"No," Terra replied. It was just the sort of life she wanted for Josh, but she didn't say so. "It helps me feel more certain that I'm doing the right thing."

Lalie gave Rafe a triumphant look. "There, Mr. Suspicious. Argue with that."

"I'd only get my knuckles rapped again," Rafe muttered. He raised a challenging eyebrow at Terra. "Aren't you on your way somewhere? Like to work?"

"Yes, and I don't need your reminder, thank you." She pushed back her chair and and went out to kiss Josh goodbye.

Then she came back in to tell Lalie she'd be back at lunchtime to pick up Josh for an hour or so.

"Kermit," Lalie said to Rafe, "would you be a gentleman and see Terra to the door?"

Rafe silently, stiffly complied, limping behind her through the living room. He undid the lock, but stopped with his hand on the knob.

"I suppose I should apologize for my attitude," he said.

"Would you mean it if you did?"

He shrugged. "Maybe. If you really meant what you said about the life I led."

"I really meant it."

He considered for a moment. "All right, then, I'm really sorry for doubting you so much."

"Nonetheless, you still do, don't you?"

"I'm starting to wish I didn't. Maybe that's what I really mean."

Terra nodded. "That's fair enough, all things considered. Maybe the longer I don't turn you in, the less you'll mistrust me. And the longer you stay put, the more I'll trust *you*."

"Could be." He blew out a long breath. "Look, if I can help Lalie out with Josh this morning—read him stories or whatever—do you have any objection?"

She could think of several objections she should have, and good reasons for them. "It probably wouldn't hurt," she replied. "Thank you for checking with me first."

"You're welcome. I'll make myself useful for a change." He turned the knob, staying completely behind the door as he opened it. "Have a nice day."

"You, too." Terra stepped out and it clicked shut behind her.

She drove away thinking, *See you at noon, I hope.*

BACK TO WORK at the resort, Terra met with Columbia in the chef's office adjacent to the kitchen. They put their heads together and sketched out a preliminary plan to produce unique, eclectic menus that would showcase regional cuisine and Columbia's creative, zestful culinary style.

It would be a challenge because the prodigious chef constantly experimented with ingredients, techniques and presentations. The menus would have to reflect her flexibility and reputation for brilliant juxtapositions of tradition, innovation and stunning surprise.

The time flew and ended too soon. Terra left Columbia's office with a heavy stack of all the menus the resort had utilized during its long history. The earliest ones were copies of originals that were now preserved in the county's historical museum. She would look through them for any design ideas they might offer.

She took the menus to her room and then called Macy to touch base. Macy reported that she was busy biting her nails about the practice projects Terra had left for her.

"Relax," Terra told her. "They're just for you to cut your teeth on, try your hand at. They don't have to be perfect."

"In my mind, they do," Macy replied, then changed the subject. "Are you having fun there, I hope?"

"More than you can even imagine."

"Any interesting men?"

"There's one who's perfect for you. The marina manager." She described Kent Prescott in enough detail to make Macy drool, then she lied. "For me, though, there's no one quite right."

"You can't make do with Kent?"

"He's much more your type than mine," Terra objected.

"So send him to San Francisco, fast," Macy said with a sigh. "My blind date is already starting to fizzle out."

After ringing off with Macy, Terra returned a few calls, then went out and got acquainted with the business center and its manager, Elise. Up-to-date office equipment was available for the guests' use, and Elise provided technical and secretarial assistance.

Terra had brought her own laptop computer, but needed a modem and printer in the hotel room. Elise arranged it all, including access to several user networks, for Terra's convenience.

While talking with Elise, Terra learned that she had a seven-year-old daughter named Caitlin. They made friendly, indefinite plans for their children to play together.

With a busy, productive morning behind her, Terra left in the golf cart to pick up Josh. She couldn't keep excitement from rising in her at the possibility that she'd see Rafe again. He was as compelling now as her memories of him had always been.

Too compelling, she told herself in a futile effort to stem her anticipation. She should be soberly contemplating the possibility that he was guilty; instead she was spinning sexual fantasies about him as she buzzed through the village.

At Lalie's a few minutes later, she knocked on the door. Lalie opened it with her finger to her lips.

"What?" Terra whispered, stepping in.

Dark eyes soft and smiling, Lalie set the lock. "Come and look."

Terra tiptoed behind her through the hall to the nap room and peeked in through a crack in the door. There on the hammock were Rafe and Josh, sound asleep. Josh lay with his head on his father's chest, one hand over the man's heart. Rafe had one arm curled around the boy, and one leg bent to prop up a storybook.

Terra caught her breath and choked up on sudden, poignant tears that gathered in her throat.

"I hate to disturb them," Lalie whispered, drawing the door shut without a creak.

Fighting for control, Terra turned away and went back to the living room on tiptoe. She took in a deep, unsteady breath, afraid to say anything and have her voice quake uncontrollably with emotion.

Lalie wiped her own eyes with a corner of her garden apron. "So heartwarming," she murmured.

Terra nodded, swallowed back the tears. "I'll leave and come back later," she managed to say.

"That's best," Lalie agreed. "I'll explain to Josh once he wakes up."

They stepped out to the front porch. Terra got a tenuous hold on control.

"When will it be safe again next door?"

"They always finish about midafternoon, then I go over to make sure the coast is clear for Rafe." Lalie crossed her fingers over her heart. "He gets lonely, though, by himself. You could probably visit him now and then over there, get to know him better."

"I'm not sure I'd be welcome."

"I have a feeling you would, but maybe you should find out for yourself."

Terra wrestled her emotions back into line during the quick drive to the resort. She'd hold in her heart forever the image of Rafe and Josh napping together, but she wouldn't let it overwhelm her. She also resolved that she wouldn't act on Lalie's suggestion to visit Rafe.

He was just too attractive and charismatic, in the flesh and in memory. In his presence she had more trouble holding a rational perspective on him than she knew she should have. So she just wouldn't visit him, period, even if he'd welcome it.

TERRA KEPT BUSY for the next little while by having lunch with Joanie in the employees' cafeteria. The concierge wasn't a gossip, but she did bring up an item of intrigue about Liz Jermain. Liz, it seemed, had a mysterious habit of suddenly slipping away for brief periods of time. Everyone suspected that she had a secret lover, but even the omnipotent Shad couldn't figure out who the mystery man was or where Liz went to rendezvous with him.

Speculating about it was a favorite pastime in the employee ranks. Nothing cruel, however, just intense curiosity.

"What are you up to the rest of the day?" Joanie asked as they left the cafeteria.

Terra replied, "Leisure activities with my son, since I promised Columbia I'd enjoy my working vacation. Josh loves the beach, which is probably where we'll spend much of our free time."

They parted in the lobby and Terra went on out to pick up Josh. She found that Rafe had gone back to the estate, which she told herself was just as well. She also found, as usual, that Rafe out of sight wasn't Rafe out of mind.

Her thoughts continued to fill with him the rest of the day. She and Josh spent it at the beach, building sand castles. That evening, they had a quiet dinner together in their room and went to bed early.

THE NEXT MORNING, before taking Josh to Lalie's, Terra got a call from Columbia.

"Bad news," the chef said. "There's a broken water pipe drowning my whole kitchen right now. Keep this afternoon penciled in, but skip it this morning. You won't ever be able to hang around and observe unless you're in waders."

"No problem," Terra told her. "I've got notes to take and photos to snap. I'll be busy."

Considering that the kitchen hardly needed two more breakfasts to put out at the moment, Terra decided that she and Josh would eat at Ye Olde Sandwich Shoppe in the village. They had a nice, comfy breakfast there and Josh made a big hit with the counterman. Then they hopped in the cart and went to drop Josh off.

Lalie was out back, snipping leaves in the herb plot when they arrived. Terra called to her as they approached. Lalie looked up and her expression showed that something was wrong.

Terra quickened her pace and hurried Josh along. When they reached her, Lalie said, "Kermit has come down with a cold this morning, so I'm cutting these herbs to make a healing tea for him." Her eyes met Terra's and signaled greater alarm than her calm tone communicated.

Terra got the unspoken message and the understanding that Lalie was keeping a lid on for Josh. For privacy, Terra sent Josh back to the golf cart to fetch her sunglasses.

As he trotted away, Lalie said worriedly, "It's the fever. Rafe's got the worst attack so far and it has laid him flat this time."

"Where is he?"

"Next door."

"How can I help, Lalie?"

"Sit with him while I brew the tea. He's half-delirious and I just hate leaving him alone, even for a minute."

"I understand." Terra was feeling alarmed herself. "Josh can play on the patio with his ball while we're both inside."

"Good idea. It's best if Josh doesn't see what chills and fever can do to a man."

Lalie finished gathering the herbs while Terra got Josh's ball. When Josh returned with the glasses, she explained to him that Kermit was visiting next door, sick with a cold, and that he needed help to get well.

Walking over to the estate, Terra instructed Josh, "Play with your ball on the patio while I help Lalie fix some tea."

"I wanna go in."

"You might catch his cold, Josh. Remember the last one you had, how stuffed up you got?"

He made a face and nodded. "I don't want that."

Terra felt chilly with apprehension as they crossed the lawn and the patio to the double doors. Josh stayed outside playing, while Lalie and Terra went in.

Rafe was on the bed, rolled up in a quilt and shivering, muttering gibberish.

"He's hot and cold by turns," Lalie said. "Tend to him while I boil up the herbs. Keep a cold cloth on his head. I'll be back." She hurried out of the room.

Terra sat in a chair that Lalie had pulled close to the bed. She removed the wet cloth from Rafe's forehead and refreshed it in a basin of ice water on the night table.

He flinched when she replaced it. She saw his eyeballs rolling wildly under his closed eyelids and then his lashes fluttered open. Eyes bloodshot, glassy and unfocused, he stared at her for a moment.

"No," he muttered through chattering teeth. "No, no, no, no."

Terra saw that he was far away from himself, unrecognizing, incoherent. Whether he was a traitor or not, he was miserably ill and needed to be cared for. She thought about what a strain the past two months must have been for Lalie. And now, Lalie had taken on the additional task of baby-sitting Josh. Perhaps she had thought that Rafe was farther along the road to recovery than he appeared to be right now. More likely, she hadn't been able to refuse without arousing Columbia's concern.

Knowing nothing about tropical fever, Terra couldn't do anything more than what Lalie had instructed. She changed the cloth again, and again Rafe flinched.

"Rafe," she murmured, touching his fiery-hot, sweat-sheened cheek, "it's me. Terra."

Strange, she thought, how they had both been knocked off their feet within the past two days.

"Terra," he mumbled. He worked one hand out of the quilt, reaching toward her.

She clasped his hand in hers. "Lalie's making you something to drink. You're not alone. You're going to feel better soon."

He seemed to calm a little from her touch and her words, so she stroked his forearm and kept speaking softly to him. He quieted a little more, eyes open and then closed again. Maintaining contact with one hand, she used her other to freshen the cloth, while telling him what she was doing and why.

He licked his lips, repeated her name in a ragged whisper and calmed down a fraction more. "Home . . . I'm home?"

"Yes. You're safe." She brought his hand to her cheek. "Relax."

His fingers spread and touched her hair. He swallowed hard, several times. "Terra . . . don't go . . ."

Lalie came in with a cup of deep green tea and Terra cradled Rafe's head as Lalie gave him a portion of the brew spoonful by spoonful. He swallowed each one mechanically, as if in a trance.

"Quinine doesn't affect it, so it's not malaria," Lalie mused. "These herbs always help, so far at least. Without a doctor to consult, folk medicine is all we've got."

Terra asked, "How long do the attacks last?"

"Anywhere from a couple of hours to half a day. This one is by far the worst."

Terra eased Rafe's head down on the pillow. Eyes closed, he reached out and clutched her hand again, as if it represented a lifeline to him. He whispered her name again, faintly.

Lalie gave a small smile. "My special angel says Kermit's finally putting some trust in you. Maybe you wouldn't mind filling my spot here while I make a quick lettuce delivery to Columbia?"

"Fine," Terra agreed, "if you'll take Josh along for the ride."

Lalie nodded. "Exactly what I was thinking. Whoever asks your whereabouts, I'll wave a hand in the air and say you're somewhere around." She left.

Terra settled more comfortably into the chair and went on stroking Rafe's hand and forearm. His breathing segued into a less labored rhythm and eased degree by degree. Then he gave a long sigh and slowly dropped off to sleep.

Terra closed her own eyes, registering the texture of Rafe's palm, the silky hair on his arm, the cooling temperature of his skin. She listened to his breath and the measured sound brought back memories of the night she spent in his arms. The night he saved her life.

7

RAFE WOKE AND FOUND himself cocooned in a quilt that he dimly remembered Lalie wrapping around him. He had only the vaguest memory of falling asleep. Now, awake, he had the tactile impression that someone was holding his hand, someone he sensed wasn't Lalie.

He slowly opened his eyes and turned his head to see who was there. Sweet Lord, yes, it was Terra Camden. Her fingers were loosely entwined with his and she had the back of his hand nestled into the warmest hollow of her lap. Her eyes were closed, but he sensed she wasn't really asleep—just resting or daydreaming.

He didn't make a sound or any further movement, but simply lay still and let his eyes fill with her. Nor did he wonder where Lalie and Josh were, or ponder whether Terra was conscious of the intimate position of his hand against her feminine mound.

It seemed he'd awakened in heaven at the end of an unplanned journey through hell. His bouts with the fever were always unpredictable. He'd never before emerged from an attack in this way, though. Never like this.

He wanted to maintain the contact, so he kept still, breathing in the subtle scent of her perfume. He lowered his gaze from her face to her breasts and lingered there for a long moment, seeing that her nipples made twin, pearl-shaped impressions against the fabric of her white blouse.

She was so feminine. And so compassionate to be there with him, caring to this extent about him.

He hadn't had this much pleasure to enjoy since . . . since the Mermaid.

Terra stirred and opened her eyes. When she saw him awake, she started and hastily transferred his hand from its nesting place to the bed.

"Oh, hi." She adjusted her blouse, clasped her hands together and cleared her throat. Then cleared it again. "Feeling better?"

Worse! he thought. *Paradise lost.* He'd been starting to feel like a million bucks before she jumped to attention and severed his heavenly connection with her. Now he got the feeling she'd been pretending he was someone else. Someone in San Francisco, probably. Someone she missed.

"I'm making a comeback," he replied defensively. "What brings you here?"

She explained where Lalie and Josh were. "You couldn't be left alone," she added.

"Sorry to inconvenience you."

He regressed to feeling surly and out of sorts, the way he always felt after a fever assault. The tropical bug in his blood was a master at ambushing him unawares, laying him flat as long as it liked, then retreating until its next spontaneous assault on him.

Lalie had tried quinine, but that hadn't worked. Without a medical professional to treat him, he was subject to the bug's whim.

The recovery period each time was surprisingly short, but the fact that the entire process would repeat without warning made him feel helpless. And angry at himself for it.

"It's not an inconvenience," Terra objected, frowning at him. "It's to help Lalie out."

"If you mean she's had it rough with me, that's easy to see."

"I mean she's been under a strain. At her age, it can't be easy to care for you and her own concerns, as well."

"You're damn right. All the more reason for me to cut out and give everybody here a big break."

"I thought we agreed that you'd stick around, Rafe."

"Temporarily agreed," he reminded her. "I'm reconsidering it."

"You're too sick to reconsider anything. Less than an hour ago you were out of it."

"I'm lucid now, thinking clearly."

"I don't think so, Rafe."

"I do," he insisted. He painfully worked his way out of the confining quilt. It was damp with sweat and the jeans he had on weren't any drier. "I'm on the mend."

She rolled her eyes. "At the very least you're dehydrated."

"Nothing a swig of water won't fix."

He swung his legs over the side of the bed and gave his all to sit up on the edge. Being weak, looking helpless, wasn't acceptable to him, especially not in front of Terra Camden.

She stood from the chair and blocked his way. "I'll get the water for you."

"I'll fare for myself, thank you very much."

He felt woozy and boneless. Not the strong, vigorous, never-sick-a-day-in-my-life type he had been a few long years ago. Not the man who could probably have attracted Ms. Camden's interest back then without a Herculean amount of effort.

He was a hollowed out shell of what he'd once been. The last thing he needed was a beautiful, caring woman putting his deficiencies into stark relief by just being there. If she'd just go away, he could ignore himself.

She said. "I'm not moving until you lie down again. You're pale, hurting, dehydrated and heaven only knows what else."

"It's nothing you can fix, okay?"

"Nokay," she replied, planting her feet wide, her hands on her hips.

Rafe figured she used that same megamom stance with her son whenever the boy kicked up a ruckus. Well, she wasn't dealing with a preschooler right now, and there was no better time than the present to make it lastingly clear to her.

He clenched his jaw and slowly came to his feet, facing her. She held her position, just a few inches away, nose to nose. She didn't blink, and neither did he. Damn if he was going to let on that he felt close to blacking out.

"Apparently, you don't comprehend what I said, Terra."

"Apparently, you don't understand what nokay means, Rafe."

"I know goddamned good and well what—"

"Don't swear."

Rafe stared down into her eyes, and she stared up into his. He clamped her upper arms in his hands, not to intimidate and subdue her, but to maintain his balance without giving away how unsteady he felt.

"I don't take orders," he told her curtly.

She countered with mock-sweet defiance, "Take a request, then. *Please*, stop swearing."

"I'll think about it."

"While you're thinking, let go of me."

"Do you agree to get out of my way?"

"Rafe, why don't you just stop this childish nonsense?"

"Oh, so you think I'm acting like Josh with the sniffles."

"Josh is a lot more reasonable when he's ill."

"Look, I didn't invite you in here, and now I'm inviting you to leave."

"You can't. This isn't your house. I'm not budging and that's final."

Rafe tightened his hold on her, and then helpless to push her out of his way, he did something he knew he'd regret later. Something he'd been wanting to do from the moment he'd first seen Terra Camden.

Slowly, giving her plenty of time to evade him if she wanted to, he bent his head and kissed her lips. To his surprise, she went still, unresisting, and let him do it. More surprising, her lips trembled under his and she made a faint, encouraging sound, then leaned into him and flattened her hands against his chest.

It took him a moment to register that her response was positive. Despite the angry words they'd flung at each other, she seemed to want the kiss as much as he did. Or was it her own stubborn way of continuing the argument? If it was, she was getting the upper hand.

Her soft, warm lips parted. Her hands slid up and curved behind his neck. He shuddered and drew her against him, then fed on her mouth with a ravenous lack of control. It had been too long, too long for him to be sane and in charge of himself. He was starved, deprived beyond any ability to hold back from taking whatever she would give.

"Kermit? Terra?" Lalie's voice stopped him like a sharp blow between the eyes.

Terra whirled away from him and physical weakness did him in again. Dizzy and shaken by too much too soon, he reeled back and dropped onto the bed.

He blinked at Lalie, who was at the patio door, poking her head inside. How long had she been there? From her bemused expression, long enough.

Her gaze swiveled back and forth between them. "What was all the shouting about?"

"Water," Rafe croaked.

Terra mumbled, "I'll get it." She hastened into the bathroom, smoothing her blouse and hair.

Lalie raised her eyebrows at him. "We're back from our delivery, Josh and I."

"C'mon in. I'm not contagious any more." Rafe slid under the soggy quilt again and sank back against the pillows.

Josh came with Lalie to the bedside. "Is your cold gone, Kermit?"

"All gone." Rafe met the boy's startling blue eyes and tried not to look fool-crazy about his mother. "What's happening with you today?"

"I got a ride. In Lalie's van."

Terra came back with a tall glass of water and kissed Josh on the cheek before setting the water on the night table. "How are you doing, big boy? Miss me?"

"I guess." He shrugged. "How come you guys yelled?"

Terra flushed and fidgeted with one of her collar points. "Um, well, Kermit's ears were plugged up from his cold and—"

"She had to yell so I could hear," Rafe finished for her. "Then I had to yell so I could hear myself. You know how it goes."

"Mmm-hmm," Lalie murmured, "sure do."

Josh settled his elbows on the edge of the mattress and studied Rafe with interest. "Do you like Power Rangers?"

Rafe had no idea what they were, but he caught Terra's prompting nod. "Do you?"

That was all it took to set Josh off, telling all about the last episode he'd seen on TV. Rafe was glad for the distraction, since it kept his immediate attention away from Terra herself. The boy had her nose, her smile and her brown hair. Except for his chin and eyes, he was his mother's son.

Josh's eyes were arresting. Even discomfiting, Rafe decided. Looking into them was a little like looking into his own eyes or his sister Liz's. The color was intense, a shade that Rafe knew from experience was often wildly attractive to people whose eyes weren't blue.

People like Terra.

She was leaving the room with Lalie, stepping out of sight to the patio. Meanwhile, Josh chattered nonstop,

punctuating his monologue with rousing, vocal sound
effects of active combat. Rafe remembered imitating
cartoon sounds as a kid and driving his parents up the
wall with the noise. *Pow! Bam! Zzzzzzzonk! Ak-ak-ak-
ak-ak-ak!*

Josh's innocent enthusiasm was infectious, bringing
back happy memories of carefree childhood days. Life
had been so simple and forthright in his boyhood.
Good was good and evil was evil and never the twain
would meet, except on the battleground where good
always won out in the end.

It was like that for Terra's little boy right now as he
recounted the exploits of the good guys against the bad
guys. Listening to him, Rafe wished that he himself had
never bought into that idealistic claptrap. He wouldn't
be where he was today if he'd been a cynic at an early
age.

Now he was a cynic at a later age, and all the worse
for it. However, he didn't want Terra's son to know how
far from ideal Kermit was. Let the kid live in the bliss
of oblivion for as long as he could, with Terra the Libra, champion of underdogs.

What had the boy's father been like, Rafe wondered. What had split Terra from him? And when? Did
she have a sweetheart in San Francisco? She hadn't
kissed like a woman who got regular, personal, male
attention. But what judge of kissing was he after five
years without even touching a woman?

"Out of it," she had said. That described him to a T
even when he wasn't down with fever.

He became aware that Josh had gone silent. The boy
was regarding him intently with a quizzical frown.

"You know my daddy?"

"No."

Josh sighed. "Me, either."

Rafe didn't know what to say, or think, whether to take the boy's words at face value or what. Never met his father? The child looked dejected, where a few moments ago he'd been charged with excitement.

"Well," Rafe finally said, "don't let it get you down. Plenty of kids never met their dads, I'll bet."

Josh brightened a little. "Really?"

"The thing is, you've got a great mom. Maybe someday you'll have a stepdad. You know kids who have them, don't you?"

"Maybe. A couple."

"Matter of fact, I've got a stepgrandfather."

"You like him?"

"I sure do."

Rafe was surprising himself with the encouraging words he found to say. An even greater surprise was the interest he took in helping the little guy sort out the issue a bit, put it in perspective.

Josh asked, "Where's *your* daddy?"

Rafe didn't really want to say, since his father and mother were dead. Charles and Vivien Jermain had died within five years of each other, a blow each time to Rafe, who had been fifteen when his mother died, twenty when his father passed away. It seemed best not to bring up such a disturbing topic, or to get mired in explanations of death and afterlife that a child wouldn't understand.

He tried an indirect reply. "My parents are together. They've got a nice place."

That was enough for Josh to drop the subject and change it entirely. "Wanna play kickball?"

"Not right now, Josh." Rafe glanced across the room. "Go see what your mom and Lalie are up to outside."

Josh ran to the door and looked through the sheers. "Blabbing. That's all."

They came inside a few moments later, looking solemn and thoughtful. Terra took Josh in hand.

"It's time we went back to the resort for lunch," she said. "Kermit needs more rest. Say goodbye."

Josh looked sad to be leaving. "Bye, sir."

"So long, mate." Rafe shifted his gaze to Terra. "For the time being, at least."

Terra didn't meet his eyes. She gave Lalie a little smile. "See you this afternoon. Around two."

WHEN THEY WERE GONE, Lalie came to the bedside chair and sat down. "Rafe," she said, "imagine if you had run out the other day and this fever hit you."

"It's a pretty sure bet I'm not running out right now," he replied.

"Don't jive me. You're thinking about it, more seriously than ever. You've got your conscience working overtime on who is involved now."

"For God's sake, Lalie, you and Terra are on the line. Without me, neither of you would have anything to fear."

"Nobody's twisting arms around here," she stated indignantly.

Rafe shook his head. "The boy's got no choice in the matter. This mess is getting out of hand."

"You got out of hand with Terra, I know. Not that she spoke a word about it to me, but I didn't miss much of the showdown you two had."

Rafe turned his face away. "Don't remind me."

She chuckled. "At least you kissed and made up at the end."

"Don't remind me about that, either."

"I won't be surprised if it happens again," Lalie mused. "Something about you two makes sense to me. Real sense."

"Nothing's going to happen if Terra stays out of here. After today, she sure as hell will."

"You think so, do you?"

"Without any doubt. By the way, what were you two so secretive about outside before she left?"

Lalie replied, "The new security system that's being installed at the resort. When I was there, Columbia mentioned security training classes that all the employees will have to take soon.

"The surveillance will be everywhere, except the village and estates. I reminded Terra to be careful wherever she is."

Rafe already knew from Lalie that Thomas Graves, the new security chief, had taken charge at the resort. Graves had moved fast from the start, beginning with a reinvestigation of every employee's security clearance. As a supplier to the kitchen, Lalie had been as closely scrutinized as the others. She'd passed muster without any problem.

Graves would have a coronary, Rafe thought, if he knew Lalie had been breaking the law, big-time, for two months now. Especially so with a Caribbean diplomats' conference coming up, not to mention the rumors of a presidential vacation on the island.

Lalie got out of her chair, ready to leave. "Rafe, try not to worry yourself sicker than you already are. And while you're at it, don't be so sure you've seen the last of Terra Camden."

"What makes you think otherwise?"

"My intuition." She went to the door. "You two would make a fine match."

AFTER SHE LEFT, Rafe settled into his pillows and pondered Lalie's words. He didn't believe her intuition, didn't want to believe they'd make a fine match.

A man with nothing to offer couldn't afford to torture himself with the idea that he'd met the woman of his dreams.

8

JOSH VOTED TO GO to the beach for lunch after leaving
Lalie's. A drinks-and-grill setup was there, serving
burgers and snacks to sun worshippers and beach-
combers. Terra brought several old menus to look
through while Josh frolicked at the surf's edge and built
sand castles. She did some people watching, too, at in-
tervals.

There were no other children, unfortunately, among
the small number of people there that day—a few cou-
ples of varying ages, a few singles, a lifeguard. One
couple's inability to keep their hands off each other
identified them as possible honeymooners. At times,
she found her attention drawn to their ardent displays
of affection toward each other.

It made her think of Rafe and what had happened to
her with him under the fresco ceiling. Maybe if she
hadn't been engrossed in a tour of memory lane when
he woke up, none of it would have occurred, neither the
confrontation nor the kiss. But engrossed she had been,
and aroused to a more than immoderate level by her
erotic memories of making love with Rafe Jermain.

She could see now that her own pent-up passion
contributed to the argument and then escalated in a
physical response that still had her trembling inside.

Although she had wanted him to kiss her, she hadn't expected that she'd put everything into it, all the passion she had in her at that electrifying moment. It had felt so good, so right, so *necessary*, at the time.

But now she felt miserably aware that she hadn't matured at all in one respect during the years between that spring break and the present. Where Rafe Jermain was concerned, she was still enchanted, still infatuated, with the same stranger in the night.

She gave a frustrated sigh and closed the menu she'd been scanning. Her gaze wandered again to the amorous couple who were suggestively positioned on a beach towel. The woman lay facedown, with her bikini top unfastened. The man knelt between her parted legs and stroked sun lotion on the skin of her back, his touch never failing to linger on the soft outer swells of her breasts.

At times, he stretched almost full-length upon her fanny and back to nuzzle her nape. Terra looked away and squeezed her eyes shut, unable to stop forming a mental image of herself and Rafe in the couple's place.

Hastily, she gathered up her homework and called to Josh. The sooner she got away from the beach, the better she'd be able to put Rafe out of her mind.

Getting her mental focus off that subject, however, proved far more difficult than deserting a torrid stretch of sand.

RAFE WAS STILL dominating her thoughts when she took Josh back to Lalie's a little after two o'clock that afternoon.

"Kermit is much improved," Lalie informed her when they got there. "Lunch did him a world of good, and maybe the special attention he got from you helped him along just as well."

Terra felt a hot flush creep up her neck to her cheeks. To cover it, she turned to Josh. "Nap time. All four-and-a-half-year-olds report to the hammock."

Josh needed no coaxing. Within a few minutes he was settled in among the stuffed animals, telling them all about life on the beach.

Terra kissed him and returned to Lalie who was dusting furniture in the living room. "Lalie," she said tentatively, "I hope you didn't get the wrong idea earlier."

Lalie raised her brows. "What wrong idea?"

"You know. Just that Rafe and I were, um, I mean..."

"Friendly," Lalie tactfully supplied.

Terra nodded, feeling as awkward and inarticulate as a schoolgirl. "That's one word for it."

"Getting as friendly as you can with each other," Lalie said, "wouldn't hurt either of you, in my opinion."

"But it would," Terra protested. "Whether he's guilty or not is still an unknown. At least to me."

"Only because you don't know him very well, yet."

"That's not the point, Lalie. You naturally think the best of him."

"Terra, I *know* the best of him. You saw my photo album of Rafe's progress through life. He needs that life back, needs to take it up where it got torn off and go on to happy years ahead. If his future includes you, so much the better."

"Me?" Incredulous, Terra blinked at her. "I'm not at all involved with him, not the way you mean."

Lalie questioned gently, "What I saw earlier wasn't love at first something?"

"Lalie, it's what got me in trouble with Rafe the first time. I've learned all I ever need to know about spontaneous combustion." She checked the time on Lalie's clock and stood. "I'd better get back to work."

Lalie saw her to the front door. "Don't mind me," she said with an apologetic sigh. "I'm an old-style romantic about some things, noticing possibilities where maybe they don't exist."

"That's all there is to it," Terra readily agreed. "I'll see you later, four-thirty or five."

She left, determined to stay away from seeing Rafe again. If Lalie needed any more help with him, she'd just have to find someone else to keep the fever watch. But who else?

BACK AT THE HOTEL, Terra went to meet with Columbia in the main kitchen. She found the chef and the kitchen crew all wearing galoshes and mopping up in the wake of a broken water pipe that had flooded the area. Liz was there, conferring with a quartet of plumbers.

Columbia withdrew from the commotion when she saw Terra and joined her on the stairs where it was dry.

"This just isn't our day, Terra. How's your jet lag?"

"Better, thanks. I'm hitting my stride, finally."

"Good, then let's meet at nine-thirty tomorrow, for sure," Columbia said, pointing out her office at the other end of the kitchen.

Terra sidestepped out of everyone's way and went back to her room. She felt somewhat at odds without Josh around, without any pressing work to do, without any real desire to swim, play golf, go horseback riding.

The beach was out of the question if the honeymooners were still there. Anyway, she wasn't in a beach mood after going there two days in a row.

She wasn't in any mood, except the only one she didn't want to be in. The one that wouldn't let up its pressure on her, and kept stepping up the tension so that her mind, heart and body were throbbing with a relentless desire to see Rafe again.

She thought of him all alone in that big house, unable to be out in the world. What did he do all day, every day? All night, every night?

She glanced at the phone, thinking, *I could call him, but not from here. From a pay phone, perhaps.* The homeowners' name, she recalled, was Hamilton. If the number wasn't unlisted, directory assistance would have it.

Terra went to the window and stared out at the peaceful, restful view of velvety lawns and moss-draped oaks. The view did nothing to calm her restlessness or stop her one-track thoughts. She couldn't shake off the idea that Rafe was only a mile away, even less distance if a person walked north from the resort beach along the sandy shore to the estate.

She would have to go and pick up Josh anyway in an hour or so....

TEN MINUTES LATER, she had changed into shorts and sandals and was dropping a coin into the pay phone at the beach grill. Information gave her the number, no problem. She dialed it, let it ring three times, hung up, dialed again.

The phone on the other end picked up. Silence.

"It's Terra," she said.

More silence, then Rafe's deep, wary voice. "Oh. Why?"

She took a deep breath. "Would you like some company for a little while?"

"Who, you?"

"Yes."

"Alone?"

"Yes, but if you wouldn't like—"

"Hold it, I would. I, uh, yeah. Where are you? I hear surf."

She explained where she was and added that she was on foot. Ignoring all the reasons she shouldn't go, she concocted a flimsy excuse. "I thought I'd beachcomb and just, well, you happen to be there along the way, so I phoned."

"Sure, sure. See you whenever you get here, I guess."

Terra hung up, figuring it would take no more than fifteen minutes to get there if she remained insane and kept a brisk pace.

LIKE A SEA HAWK, Rafe watched the view through the kitchen window. He almost flattened his nose against the pane to get the closest possible outlook across the long stretch of property between the house and the shore. The beach itself wasn't visible from anywhere in the home, except maybe the roof peak, but as soon as Terra reached the top of the stone steps leading up to the yard, he'd see her.

She'd be framed against the ocean blue—a welcome sight. Too damned welcome. But he hadn't let that stop him when she called. His jaw had almost broken from its drop to the floor when he'd picked up the phone and heard her warm, sexy voice on the other end.

He still couldn't quite believe she had phoned, that she was coming. Company for a little while. There was a lot of company he'd readily turn down, but not hers. Not now.

He promised himself he'd turn it down after this one time. Not that he thought there'd be any time after this that she'd call. Especially not if she was coming over to give him a piece of her mind about his behavior earlier in the day.

At the moment, though, he wouldn't even mind being chewed out. He'd apologize right away, the minute she got inside.

If she really was coming. It seemed like hours since her call. Smart of her to use the pay phone at the grill. It gave him a glimmer of faith that she really didn't want to see him get caught.

Or was he the world's biggest fool for believing she'd show up without a squadron of federal agents? With his life on the line, he couldn't give anyone but Lalie his full trust. He was paranoid, but under the circumstances he had to be.

He'd know soon enough if Terra had company with her, but God help him, he believed she was coming by herself.

All by herself.

His heart lost a beat as she came into view at the top of the steps. The sun was in her eyes and she shaded them with one hand, even though she was wearing sunglasses. The gesture brought her breasts to his rapt attention. She was wearing a pink T-shirt, boat-necked, full of feminine curves. It was tucked into white Bermuda shorts. Her shiny, breeze-blown hair had an auburn sheen in the sunlight.

Rafe swallowed hard, watching her graceful legs carry her closer and closer. She gave a hesitant little wave when she spotted him at the window and her mouth curved in a half smile. Closer and closer. Still by herself.

Rafe knew he wanted Terra Camden too badly to be inviting her in with him. And nothing on earth could stop him from deactivating the security alarm and opening the door for her when she got there.

"Hi," she said breathlessly.

It gave him the idea that either she had rushed all the way, or the feds would explode out of the hedges in the next three seconds. The moments passed without incident, though, giving him time to reset the alarm.

He cleared his throat. "Nice of you to call."

"Well, it was just a sudden thought," she said, storing her sunglasses on her hair like a headband.

For several ticking seconds then, they stood looking at each other, tongue-tied.

"Sudden thought," he repeated idiotically.

She nodded slowly. "Spur of the moment. You know."

Rafe only knew that he wanted her company, her voice, the scent of her perfume in the air. Beyond that, he wanted to carry her off to the bedroom and keep her there for the next hundred years. But even if she'd let him sweep her off her feet, his back and bum knee would sabotage any romantic effort.

He wasn't what he'd once been. Might never be again.

"Anything you'd like to do?" he heard himself say. "I mean, drink."

"No, thanks. I called because, um, actually, I'd sort of like to apologize."

"So would I."

"I got a little too bossy," she said. "About nothing, really."

"Well," he said, "I showed too much of my stubborn streak. And kissing you was out of line, too."

A soft smile curved her lips. "I think I participated as much as you did."

"You're not going to slap my face and call me a barbarian?"

She shook her head. "No. In fact, I wouldn't mind sitting down somewhere and just . . . well, visiting for a while until it's time to get Josh."

"Neither would I," he assured her, leading the way out of the kitchen to the parlor. Going ahead of her, he hated for her to see his leg gimp and his back crick. He could just imagine the able-bodied males she'd observed on the beach today. Some contrast he was to them. Still, she was here, not there, which meant something. He wasn't sure what.

Terra took a seat at one end of an antique Italian sofa. He chose the opposite end to keep himself a little more sane about her than he'd be if he sat closer.

"I promise to be more civil from now on," he said. "Isolation gets to me, I guess."

She tucked one leg under her and angled herself to face him. "I understand. I mean, all things considered, I don't blame you for doing your best to shut me up."

"My best," he scoffed. "Before my whole life went to hell, I'd have sweet-talked you into not arguing with me. This morning, I—" He broke off and shook his head at himself. "Listen, I'm as sorry as can be."

"Me, too. Enough said on both sides." She sighed, as if with relief. "I'm glad I dropped by. Anyway, aside from wanting to say what I've already said, I was also wondering how you are."

"Not racked with fever, thankfully. And thanks for your help."

"You're welcome. It was no bother."

He gave her a mock-cynical smile. "Great rapport we're building with each other."

"You said the same thing the other day for vastly different reasons," she said, returning the smile.

Another silence lengthened between them, far less awkward than the previous gap in the kitchen. It was punctuated by the measured tempo of a grandfather clock in a corner of the room.

"So," he finally said, "are you working hard at the resort?"

"Hardly." She explained that the afternoon hadn't gone as planned.

"Have you met my sister yet?"

"Briefly. She's very impressive."

"I miss her." He felt his throat clutch and wondered why he was suddenly showing his deeper emotions. Yet, he went on. "I miss my whole family. Lalie keeps me filled in on everyone, though. It helps to know, at least."

"Yes." Terra nodded, her expression solemn. "It must. Family is all-important."

"What about yours?" He was more curious than he should be.

Terra told him a little about them. Army. Chaplains. Retired from service. "They wouldn't believe what I've gotten into here," she concluded. "Not for a minute."

Rafe said, "I have big trouble believing it myself."

"You still don't trust me very much."

He didn't reply.

"Well?"

"Look, what do want me to do, lie? You've got my life in your hands and I don't have any control over it."

"You really can trust me, Rafe."

"What's in it for you, Terra? Besides protecting Lalie, I mean."

She looked away. "Who knows? Anyway, turning you in would inevitably lead to Lalie—not that she isn't breaking the law, but I can see why she is. Her motives aren't criminal."

"Yours aren't, either," he said, "if it's Lalie you're most concerned about."

"I'm concerned about you, too, Rafe. If you're innocent, you need the chance to prove it."

He raised his eyebrows. "'If.' Maybe I can't prove it. What then?"

"Maybe you can and will."

"This is a chancy game you're playing with my life, Terra."

"Game!" She jumped to her feet, angered by the word. "I take back my apology to you. You're rude, arrogant, hostile and a thousand more negatives I could think of if I wanted to waste that much time."

"You're not the only one who can cancel an apology," he snapped. "I'm not sorry that I kissed you."

"I am. It seems to be the only way you could stop losing the argument we had."

"I wasn't losing."

"You are now."

He stood slowly, painfully, but not without a comeback to her words. "Good night, then."

"I don't see anything good about it," she retaliated. "You know what's wrong with you?"

"Wrong?" He blurted out his next words before he could bite them back. "You're my big problem—too much of everything I ever wanted in a woman."

She went silent for what seemed like several minutes, even though the clock marked only a few seconds.

"You're what's wrong with me, too," she said in a low, thrumming tone. "It's an attraction I can't handle."

Rafe's anger slammed to a stop. He felt sure he hadn't heard her correctly. She couldn't have said that. Not that.

"What?"

"Never mind." She darted a skittish, evasive glance at the clock. "It's time to get Josh."

Rafe touched her arm. "Hold it."

"No, I'd better leave." She brushed him off and moved past him to leave the room. "I shouldn't have come over here. Getting any more involved with you isn't the answer to anything."

Rafe caught up to her at the parlor doorway. He wrapped his hand around her elbow and stopped her there. "Wait a minute, Terra. I'm your big problem the same way you're mine?"

"Unfortunately, you are," she replied, her cheeks flushed with color, her eyes avoiding his. "It's more of a problem every time I see you."

"I had no idea," he murmured.

Terra leaned back against the doorframe and shut her eyes. "It's not an attraction that either of us needs."

Rafe eased his hold on her elbow and skimmed his fingertips over the soft skin of her arm down to her hand. "It's got a bigger grip on me than I can handle, Terra. You're right that I don't trust you, but the way I want you is something else."

Eyes still shut, she gave a tremulous sigh, slipping her fingers into the spaces between his. "Rafe, I really need to go. If I stay much longer, I'll lose all my good sense."

Rafe knew he should let her go, hold himself back from receiving the hesitant message her touch was sending to him, yet he couldn't force himself to release her hand. Instead, he curled his fingers tightly around hers. He heard her breath quicken. She murmured his name and it undermined his control.

"We'll both lose," he agreed.

She nodded, forehead against his chin. "It's probably nothing more than sexual attraction."

"No." He stepped closer, needing to feel her body against his. "It's more than lust. Terra, don't leave just yet."

He couldn't release her now that he knew she had feelings so much like his. She was right that it was the last thing they needed, that they should resist what was drawing them together. Whatever it was. Even so, he was elated to discover that the feeling was mutual.

Rafe told himself he'd work up the necessary resistance, but not until *after* another kiss. One to go on, that was all. Then their brakes would function, they'd both stop, she'd walk out the door and that would be the end of it.

"Rafe, I've got to go now, right n—"

He stopped her words by lifting her hand to his lips. Her other hand came up to his chest, to rest over his heart. His free hand found its way around her waist to where the small of her back pressed against the doorframe. She made a helpless sound and arched toward him, allowing his fingers and then his forearm into the space.

One step brought them toe-to-toe, his body against hers, and he could tell it wasn't lost on her that he was aroused. He wished he could regret it, but he didn't.

"Don't go yet," he whispered against the fragrant, silky skin on the back of her hand. "In a minute."

"A minute," she agreed in a faltering whisper and then a heartbeat later she was mouth-to-mouth with him, giving him open encouragement, taking in his tongue the moment he thrust it past her lips and teeth.

She made a soft, quiescent sound in the depths of her throat and Rafe realized right away that they'd both made a huge mistake. His own need was too great for him to be satisfied with only a kiss, no matter how lengthy or explicit it became. And Terra's response was no less intemperate, no less rife with frustration.

He felt her lower body welcome the pressure of his desire for her. Shifting her hips against him, she made a soft, undulating delta of encouragement for him where his hand had nestled yesterday. If they'd both been undressed right then, he could have slipped partway into her.

The erotic awareness made him shake, made him groan as he kissed her, made him hurt even worse to make love with her. She wanted it, too, he could feel how much from the way her tongue was matching his stroke for stroke, the way she trembled in his arms and moved her hips in rhythm with his.

He touched her breast and she made another, deeper sound as his quivering fingers radiated apart to contain her full, firm shape. Against his palm, her nipple was taut, an electrifying point of sensation.

Gong! The clock struck loudly and startled them apart. They stared at each other, gasping, while it tolled four more times.

As the chimes echoed into silence, Terra drew a deep, unsteady breath and slowly pushed him away until he backed up against the opposite doorframe.

"What are we doing?"

Rafe caught his own ragged breath and replied, "Kissing goodbye, I think."

"Goodbye," she repeated, looking confused and flushed. "Yes, I was leaving, I—" She broke off and put her hands to her flaming cheeks. "God, why did you do that, Rafe?"

"Do what?"

"Kiss my hand like you did. Why didn't you just—" Breaking off again, she clenched her teeth and gave a soft, frustrated groan.

"I want you," he said frankly. "I can't help it or hide it right now."

She stepped away and headed toward the kitchen. "I'm not coming back here, no matter what."

Following behind her, Rafe said nothing. He wanted her to come back and he was afraid he'd beg her to if he opened his mouth. All around, it would be best if she stayed away—best for both of them. The situation was complicated enough without stirring a heated attraction into it.

It wasn't just sexual, either, he instinctively recognized. He couldn't say precisely how he knew, but he had a certainty that Terra didn't take tumbles for cheap thrills. She wasn't the type, and he'd been around too much not to trust his instincts in that one respect. She was the type to put emotion into her passion. Quality emotion.

As to why she'd showed passion toward him, he didn't have any instincts at all that answered the question. On that score, he was in the dark, wondering. And hurting so bad. Jeez, he was embarrassed to be so out of control.

Terra reached the kitchen door a step ahead of him. She didn't turn around to look at him when she got there. Eyes straight ahead of her, she spoke. "Again, I'm sorry. It wasn't my original intention to come here and get reckless."

He nodded, even though she had her back to him and couldn't see. "You thought I'd be more of a gentleman than I was," he said.

"No, that I'd be more of a lady." Her shoulders slumped. "So much for knowing myself."

Rafe kept silent, willing her to look over her shoulder at him. After a few seconds, she half turned and met his eyes.

"Look," he said, "it took two to tango. Granted, it's the last thing we should have been doing, but it happened." He ran a hand through his hair and rubbed the back of his neck with the heel of his palm. "No more regrets, okay? We've got enough on both sides here."

She nodded, then gave the security alarm keypad a glance that prompted him to enter the code and open the door for her.

"So long, Terra," he murmured.

She smiled ruefully, pausing on the first step. "So long, yourself. Stay out of trouble, if you can."

"Don't send me any if you can help it," he returned, forcing himself to sound nonchalant about not seeing her again when in truth he felt downhearted as hell about it.

She didn't cast a backward look at him, as she continued out and disappeared around the corner of the house on her way next door.

Rafe closed the door and set the alarm. *End of love story,* he thought. Not that he was actually in love with Terra. He should be thankful for that, he told himself, since it would be easy to go whole heart for her. Far more than a physical chemistry, love would be the worst complication for him right now.

Love. He couldn't imagine why the word had popped into his mind, nor did he want it there. Now that he'd thought of it, however, he couldn't force it out.

Rafe wandered back into the parlor and found the fragrance of Terra's perfume lingering in the air. He skimmed his fingers under his nose and smelled the scent they'd picked up from her, floral and feminine, romantic and . . . riveting.

It was too potent a reminder of her, and he shouldn't be standing there breathing it in, torturing himself with every little thing he could remember about her.

The thing to remember was she wouldn't be back. She had a life that included a precious child, a satisfying career, loving parents, a happy world of her own. She didn't need a prison-scarred, isolated fugitive casting a shadow over it all.

So, she wouldn't be back. She'd be near, but not here. He'd get used to it, he told himself. He'd have to.

9

FOR NEARLY A WEEK, Terra stayed strictly away from
Rafe. She didn't speak of him to Lalie, and Lalie said
nothing about him either, as if she knew he was a sore
subject. Only Josh brought up Kermit, far too often for
Terra's comfort.

She worked a portion of each day with Columbia
and gradually the menu project began taking on the
shape and unique detail they were striving to achieve.
Terra used the business center's desktop publishing
equipment to work out a variety of sample menus with
varying themes, color schemes and fold combinations
for comparison. There were daily and seasonal menus,
ones for holidays, catered affairs, special events.

In her off time, she and Josh enjoyed beachcombing,
horseback riding, hiking in the forest preserve. They
rode the ferry to Charleston one afternoon and took a
sight-seeing bus tour of the city. Twice they picnicked
with Elise and her daughter at an old lighthouse on the
southern tip of the island.

Every day, Terra halfway expected Lalie to an-
nounce that Rafe had flown the coop. But the days
passed without that happening.

Then, at the start of Terra's second week there, Lalie
surprised her. They'd settled Josh down for his nap and
Terra was ready to leave. Lalie handed her a sealed en-

velope that had no writing on it, no stamp, no postmark. "Some mail for you, Terra."

Terra took it gingerly, knowing without having to ask who'd sent it. She turned it over and over in her hands. "What if I don't want to hear from him?"

"Terra, if I believed that, I wouldn't be playing pony express."

"What does he want?"

"Good question." Lalie tactfully turned away and busied herself with straightening a picture on the wall.

Terra hesitated, biting her lip. Then she broke the seal and opened the envelope. Inside was an invitation to a swim party. The date: any day. The time: anytime. The host: Kermit. RSVP: please.

Silently she showed it to Lalie, who said, "It would do you both good."

"Lalie, I told him I wasn't going back there. He agreed that I shouldn't."

"Then write him your regrets and I'll see that he gets it. Or should I just hurt his feelings and tell him you refuse to change your mind?"

"What about my own feelings? He's not taking me at my word."

"He's taking up trust in you. He misses seeing Josh too, I believe, after spending that little time with him."

"I don't want to get any more involved."

"Okay. Do you tell him or do I tell him?"

"I will. I'll call."

"Do it from here while I cut some herbs you can take to Columbia when you go back."

She went out to the garden and Terra used the wall phone in the kitchen. As before, Rafe didn't say a word when he picked up the receiver on the other end.

"It's me."

"Oh. Long time."

"About the party..."

"Well?"

"You know it's not a good idea."

Silence.

"Can you hear me?"

"I hear you're not coming any day, anytime." His voice cracked on the last word and he paused to clear his throat. "Right?"

"No—I mean, uh, I am, but is Josh invited, too?"

"Sure." His words tumbled over one another. "Absolutely. Both of you, for sure."

"Um, how about later this afternoon, then? Three-thirty?"

"I'll be here."

"Which door?"

"Patio."

He clicked off abruptly, as if afraid that she'd change her mind. Terra hung up the receiver and leaned her forehead against it. She closed her eyes, acknowledging to herself that she was just helpless about Rafe Jermain. The past several days had been a trial, costly to her self-control, ravaging it.

All he probably wanted was company to ease his loneliness, and a warm body to reduce his natural frustration level, she argued with herself. She was familiar enough with her own stifled libido not to blame him for having the same problem.

Taking Josh along would keep her on the straight and narrow with Rafe this afternoon. Alone with him, she wouldn't have a chance. Josh would enjoy the indoor pool, and so would she, even though her tension level wouldn't let up around Rafe.

Luckily, she had conquered her fear of water and learned to swim after Josh was born. He had learned along with her at the same time, and now he was a great little paddler, comfortable in any depth. He'd have great fun, especially with Rafe. Daddy.

Her thoughts were cut short as Lalie came in with a basket of fragrant, fresh-cut herbs. "What makes me think you didn't say no to that party, Terra?"

"Maybe the worried look on my face?"

Lalie beamed. "Some things are just meant to be, I always say."

"You're too much of an old-style romantic, Lalie. This is serious trouble I'm getting into and you're no help. You're egging me on."

"Take Josh with you if you want to keep in the shallow end at the party."

"I've already arranged that little safety guard." Terra took the basket, ready to leave. "I'll be back to get him at three-thirty."

"And when is the party?"

"Same time."

Lalie chuckled, then laughed and laughed.

"It's not *that* funny," Terra grumbled, going out the front door. "Or else your sense of humor is warped."

She couldn't help breaking into a warped smile at herself, though. Impetuous and impatient had never been her middle names, but who would believe it to-day?

There was still time to call the whole thing off.

Nevertheless, Terra dressed in a buttercup yellow tank swimsuit and covered it up with a terry-cloth tunic. She packed towels and Josh's swimsuit into a beach bag, slung it over her shoulder and left her room.

Time remained for her to change her mind as she passed through the lobby. All she'd have to do was pick up the pay phone in the rest-room alcove, plunk in a coin and hurt Rafe's feelings.

Nevertheless, she went out to her golf cart and left the resort. In the village, she slowed down at the gas station pay phone, her next-to-last chance to cancel out. She almost came to a stop, but then quit dithering and drove on to collect her son.

Josh was beside himself with excitement when she arrived. He dug his swimsuit out of the bag and ran inside to change. Terra thought of all the explaining she'd have to do if her exhausted self-control revived before time ran out. She still had a minute or two left to call Rafe from Lalie's phone, but Josh was so keyed up he'd throw a hellacious fit if she backed out now.

He came speeding back out in record time, a quick-change champ. She was committed. She had to face it. Lalie was humming a cheerful tune while watering radicchio lettuce, and there was nothing else to do but show up next door in a swimsuit, with a smile.

Terra gave a wave to Lalie and turned Josh loose. "Ready, set, go."

He ran through the gate and over the lawn to the patio. Following behind him at a slower pace, Terra saw the door open and admit him into the bedroom. She drew a deep breath as she approached the entrance. A few more steps and she was inside, face-to-face with a man she was falling in love with, her son's father, the man she couldn't make herself leave alone.

He wasn't wearing much, just a summer shirt, unbuttoned down the front, and slim-cut black swim trunks. He gave her a slow smile and politely took the beach bag from her.

"Miss me as much as I missed you?"

She hedged, "It's been a while, Kermit."

He seemed to have gained a little weight and looked less pale. His eyes had a vibrant hue, which intensified as they held hers.

"You're looking good, Terra."

"You, too."

He shrugged. "It's been slow going. More of that blasted fever."

Josh impatiently tugged the hem of Rafe's shirt. "Where's the pool?"

Rafe took them through a wing of the house that Terra hadn't seen before—a family room, solarium and finally to the indoor pool. It was L-shaped, aquamarine, rimmed at the waterline with hand-painted Mediterranean tiles. Half-circled around it were lush tropical plants and palms.

Josh squealed and plunged right in with a big splash. Rafe set the tote down and shrugged off his shirt. Terra did her best not to reveal that the dark hair on his chest made her fingertips restless to roam through it. Nor as if his snug trunks drew her interest and stopped her breath.

She got the air moving through her lungs again and said, "Your knee seems to be doing better."

He nodded. "Some ways I'm improving. Even my back, although I'm not fit to dive off the deep end yet."

"C'mon, you guys," Josh called to them.

Rafe went to the steps end and waded in, then ducked beneath the surface and swam up under Josh.

Terra slipped off her tunic and dove in. She swam a few leisurely laps while the boys tussled and splashed each other. Their playful, affectionate togetherness touched her, brought poignant tears to her eyes for the family they were and yet couldn't be. She let the tears spill, for they left no trace in the water, and the chlorine could be blamed for red eyes.

Once past the keen edge of emotion, she rested on a step in the shallow end. Rafe came over to sit with her. Together, they watched Josh as he repeatedly got out of the water and plunged back in.

Rafe chuckled. "He's too much. Does he ever wear out?"

"It'll be a while yet before he runs down," Terra replied with a fond smile at her son. "Fresh from his nap and raring to go."

Rafe propped his elbows on the step behind him, easing his spine against it. "So," he said, "what's new with you?"

"Nothing, really. Between work and play, time marches on."

He said, "Last week you didn't tell me you had dinner with Miz Elizabeth and Judge Bradshaw."

"I was afraid it would make you miss them."

"Lalie filled me in after talking to Columbia." He smiled. "I even heard about the Scuppernong Jam Cake."

"A lucky break," Terra demurred.

"My grandmother's a true believer in you now. I can see why, too."

Terra ducked the compliment. "It's interesting work."

"You're an interesting woman, Terra."

She slid a sideways look at him. "To a captive audience, perhaps."

"You'd interest me just as much if I had all the freedom I had before." He gave a harsh sigh. "God only knows if I'll ever be a free man again, though . . . free to walk the streets . . . free to fall in love."

His hand dipped under the surface and covered hers on the step. She thrilled at the contact, but nevertheless set up a verbal roadblock. "Love is something we should leave out of the conversation, Rafe."

"Sorry, Terra, but it's there. At least for me."

She did her best to resist. "We'd be crazy to get any more involved than we are. We both know—"

He put a finger to her lips and stopped her. "I know it's more than lust between us. Something more..." He tipped her chin up and gazed deeply into her eyes. "Or am I speaking only for myself?"

"No," she breathed. "But even so, we aren't free to pursue it."

He said, "Before long, I'll have my only shot at clearing my name. If I pull it off, where would you stand with me?"

"Rafe, you were a rover before everything happened. Wouldn't you return to life at sea if your options opened up again?"

He drew his hand away from her chin and pulled back a little. "It's the only life I know—man and the sea, me and my boat. Sure."

"It's not the life for me, Rafe. I have Josh, a settled life, my own business."

"We're opposites, you mean."

She nodded. "Maybe that's the big attraction, instead of anything else."

"Maybe not, Terra." He pulled farther away and settled back against the step again, looking distant and unhappy. Then, abruptly, he changed the subject. "Josh mentioned his dad to me last week."

Terra tensed. "Oh? What about him?"

"Nothing, if you don't want to talk about it."

"It's irrelevant." She detached her hand from his.

"Josh seemed to need some male advice."

"About what?"

"I assured him you'd probably get married someday and then he'd have a stepfather. Sort of like I have a stepgrandfather. He perked up and that was all there was to it."

Terra pictured the two of them having their boy-to-man, heart-to-heart conversation. Tears threatened again, tears she clamped back.

"Maybe I will, you never know," she managed to say.

"What happens until then, Terra?"

"For the present, I battle my attraction to you."

"Any chance you'd stop battling?" His hand reached to hers once more. Again, his mere touch made her melt inside.

"Have a brief affair with you, in other words."

"If you want to call it that," he said. His gaze straying to her breasts had the impact of a caress.

Terra felt her nipples ache and tighten and knew the stretch fabric of her swimsuit didn't compress the response. She couldn't dispute Rafe's words with her body speaking the visible truth.

"I brought Josh along to prevent that," she said. "To keep me sensible." She started to slide her hand away from his, but he caught it back.

"Holding hands won't hurt, Terra. Nothing steamy." His fingers slid between hers in a loose clasp.

"Rafe, we both remember how steamy we got before. We both have to hold back or we'll be in too deep with each other before we know it."

"You're afraid I'm guilty, aren't you?"

"I'm hopeful that you aren't."

"But not certain," he said. "That's the big holdup with you."

"Rafe, you didn't disagree with me that getting together wasn't a plus for us."

"Well, I'm not as averse to it as I was. I mean, if you were sure of my innocence, what would you do now?"

"Before I'd know, I'd have to be sure."

"Would you help me to prove myself if you could?"

"Help how?"

He took a deep breath. "The plan I mentioned the first day. I've been biding my time, getting well so I'll have the strength I need when the time comes. But time's getting short. I can't carry it out alone."

"What *is* the plan?"

"The part I need you for is transportation. I want to go into Charleston one night, possibly two. Find out a few things, even though it would be dangerous. I need a motorboat, which is where you come in. You could rent one from the hotel marina. Lalie couldn't do it without there being questions, because she's not keen on boating. No one would question you, though."

"I've never done any boating before."

"The marina gives lessons if guests need them. A couple of hours with Kent Prescott would get you up to speed in the waters around the island, since he knows this area as well as I do. He should, he was my best friend."

"I didn't know that."

"Maybe he still is. I don't know. Anyway, check with him."

"What reason would I give for taking a boat out at night?"

"You want to sample some Charleston nightlife, maybe, and don't want to be tied to the ferry schedule. Who wouldn't understand that? You take the boat out, bring it around here to me and no one's any the wiser. No questions asked. No suspicions aroused. It's better than if I steal a boat from one of the other estates."

Terra considered what he'd said. "Once you have the boat, you go to Charleston." A chilling, cautionary thought came to her. "Or is that just what you want me to believe? Are you going to disappear, like you wanted when I first knew about you?"

"No." His mouth and eyes hardened. "It's not an escape scheme. I wouldn't use you like that, believe me."

"Rafe, you've only told me part of the plan. What is the rest of it?"

"You don't need to know. If it works or doesn't work, you'll hear it on the news."

"When?"

"The less you know now, the better for you."

"It keeps me torn between believing and disbelieving you."

"Look, all I've got going for me is you and Lalie. If there was any other way, I'd leave you out of the plan entirely." He glanced at Josh with a pained look. "Do you think I like endangering and incriminating the mother of a small child?"

"No, but—"

"Forget it," he cut in curtly. "Forget everything I said. I'll steal a boat if I have to." He pulled his hand away from hers, ducked below the surface and swam underwater toward Josh.

It reminded Terra of the night he'd saved her life. He hadn't questioned anything when he'd cut through the dark water and rescued her. No questions asked, he'd just done all that he could to help. Didn't she owe him that now?

Steadied by that thought, she pushed off and swam after him. Catching up after he surfaced near Josh, she touched his shoulder. He turned, his eyes a deep and churning blue.

"Let's talk about my part in it tomorrow," she said. "Just the two of us."

"Don't say it if you don't mean it, Terra."

"Expect me at three-thirty, same as today. The patio door."

"Leave your worst suspicions behind if you come."

"I'll do my best." She managed a small, wry smile and repeated his own words to him. "Believe me."

"Okay. Three-thirty."

10

THE NEXT MORNING, Terra looked up Kent Prescott at the marina. She asked about boat rentals and lessons, prices and procedures. He gave her a brochure with all the information she needed, and told her he'd be glad to teach her the basics of motorboating.

She promised to get back to him later about it, and went on to work. The hours until three-thirty seemed to drag, even though she kept busy. She had a meeting with Columbia and Liz first. Then a coffee break with Joanie and Elise, lunch with Josh in the village and a sauna session at the resort health club after that to relax.

She'd told Lalie, but not Josh, where she'd be later in the day. Lalie had smiled encouragingly and said, "Wherever your heart leads you."

When the time finally approached, Terra changed into a shell pink sundress with a ballet-length swirl skirt. Anticipating that Rafe would like the dress, she slipped into sandals and sprayed on a light mist of perfume.

Checking her appearance in the mirror, she saw that her cheeks were flushed with excitement. Rafe had that effect on her, despite all her reasons for trying to shore up her resistance to him. It was crumbling fast, and knowing she'd be alone with him this afternoon keyed her up beyond thinking she could resist any longer.

Walking along the beach to Rafe's hideaway, she knew there was no doubt of where her heart was leading her. None at all.

RAFE WAS AT THE DOOR when she got there. He let her in and didn't say a word at first. His eyes said it all. Burning blue, they took in her face, her dress, her straw tote and sandals, telling her he desired her.

She saw that his jeans and T-shirt were freshly washed. He was barefoot, standing tall, radiating masculine sex appeal.

"Do you mind if I stare?" he inquired huskily.

She replied, "I think I'd mind if you didn't," and made a slow turn to show off the dress and maybe to communicate more than words could say. "How are you?"

"Fine, now that you're here." He gestured at the seating area across the room. "I borrowed a white burgundy from the wine cellar. Would you like some?"

She nodded, seeing the bottle and glasses on a teak table between two love seats. He led her there and sat down beside her. After pouring the wine, he made a toast.

"To beautiful, beautiful you."

"Thank you, handsome."

He gave a self-conscious shrug. "Tell me that when I'm down with fever the next time."

"I hope there isn't a next time, Rafe. For your sake."

"Me, too," he said, touching his glass to hers again. "Hold that hope."

His fingers brushed hers and the contact struck a charged silence between them. She drew a sharp breath and he leaned a little closer.

"Um, about renting a boat," she said, stalling for time to decide what she'd do—or wouldn't do—if he kissed her.

"What about it?"

"I checked with Kent. It looks doable, so I'll do it."

He took her free hand in his. "I'm sorry it has to be you. If I get caught in it, I'll say I stole it."

"I hope you don't get caught, Rafe."

"There's another hope to hold." His thumb rubbed warm, stimulating circles in her palm. "I'm going to miss you after you leave next week."

"I'll miss you, too."

He set down his glass and drew her toward him by the hand. "Terra, come here. I need more than to talk about boats today. Don't you?"

She nodded, and put down her own glass next to his with trembling fingers. "I do, Rafe."

She leaned forward, seeking a kiss, and got what she wanted. His lips on hers, hot and heedless, desperate with need. His hands holding her head. His fingers flexing in her hair.

She wouldn't keep herself back now, wouldn't interfere with her overwhelming feelings for her first lover, her child's father. She would give to him now, and take from him, with nothing in mind but the passion that was sweeping her away with him.

Rafe murmured her name upon her lips and rimmed them with his tongue. He sank back into the corner of the love seat, taking her with him, into his arms, holding her as if he'd never let go. Her hand on his chest felt the vibrant drumbeat of his heart. Tummy against his lower body, she felt him throb and harden.

Thrilled by his response, she pressed all the more tightly against him and then pulled back slightly to gaze into his eyes. They were heavy lidded, gleaming with desire, but there was also a shadow of hesitation.

"Terra, I might be a disaster. My back, my knee, you know?"

"We'll work it out," she predicted softly, surely, without any doubt that their need for each other would more than compensate.

He groaned, bending his head to her, his lips capturing hers again. Terra rose slowly from the love seat with him and stood for everlasting moments in his arms, wrapped close against his tall, aroused body, sharing a deep, wondrous kiss.

Urgently, his tongue moved against hers, sent heat roiling into her blood. Fingers shaking, he lowered the delicate straps of her dress and kissed her bare shoulders, heated her skin with his rushing breath.

She shimmied with pleasure and arched up for him to peel the top of her dress down. Hands flat against his T-shirt as she offered herself to him, she brushed her fingertips over the white fabric and found the tiny, stiff points of his nipples.

"God, Terra," he whispered, touching her the same way. "You don't know what you do to me."

She sighed, loving his husky whisper and the ardent tremor in his fingers as he caressed her. "I know what *you* do to me," she assured him softly.

Breathing hard, he lowered her bodice, his eyes savoring the soft upper swells of her breasts. Slowly, he bared her, and his mouth swooped down, taking in one pink peak and then the other.

"Yes," she sighed, her nipples so sensitive and responsive to him.

His hot eager mouth devoured her and his hands pushed the dress farther down, past her waist and hips until it fell to the floor. Terra stepped out of her sandals and the pool of pink fabric, at the same time helping Rafe skin off his shirt and jeans.

"Rafe," she whispered, sliding her fingertips through the crisp, dark hair on his chest, finding his nipples again, touching her tongue to them.

He clasped one hand in her hair, tipping her head back to take her mouth in a driving, yearning kiss, while his other hand cupped her bottom and lifted her against him.

Together, they moved to the bed, taking off her panties and his briefs in reckless haste. Once on the bed it didn't matter to either of them that Rafe had to sit up against the headboard because of his sprained back. Nothing mattered but the closeness they were sharing, the intimacy they both craved.

Terra straddled his thighs and linked her hands behind his neck. He filled his hands with her breasts, whispering, "Perfect, like you."

They took up once more, kissing, caressing, nipping, nibbling, gently sucking and biting. Terra sighed with rapt pleasure as Rafe's fingers parted the moist petals between her open thighs and stroked her. The pleasure was so exquisite she rose to her knees, rocking against his hand.

She gave back by curling her hand around his erection and stroking him at the same time. Gently, because he warned her he couldn't take very much.

"Terra." He eased her hand away from him. "You aren't protected are you?"

"No." Embarrassed that she hadn't considered any consequences, she blushed. "I didn't think I'd . . . we'd get carried away."

"It's all right, we're covered." He opened the bedstand drawer and took out a condom.

Relief flooded her, and desire rushed in again as she helped him put on the sheath. Then there was nothing to hold back as Rafe cupped his palms around her bottom and guided her hips down to take him in.

She settled slowly, gently, to spare him, and when finally he was sheathed in her to his full extent, she kept still, gripping his shoulders, gazing into his eyes.

She could have whispered right then that she loved him, because she did, heaven help her. He was the only man for her, right or wrong, guilty or innocent. He had been the only one from the moment he saved her from drowning.

And now she was in love with him, awash in passion for him, holding him deep inside where their child had come to life.

"Rafe," she gasped, reflexively tightening her heat around him, then fitting her mouth to his and taking more pleasure still from his thrusting tongue.

He moaned and thrust up, time and again until her first spasm seized her. Then his hips rolled hard and fast as the explosive rapture took her, shook her, blew her away. With a radiant cry, she arched her spine and threw her head back, shuddering, bursting within, again and again.

Rafe gave way with an ecstatic shout, pulsing inside her until they were both breathless, dazed and spent.

LATER, AS THEY LANGUISHED in contentment, Rafe pressed his lips to her tousled hair. Head on his shoulder, she lay half beside and half on him, snuggled against him.

He chuckled softly. "I think you fixed my back."

"For the worse, no doubt," she murmured, twining her fingers in the hair on his chest.

"Really, it feels better. That one spot that hurt so badly all the time."

Terra trailed her fingers down to his naval and teased the rim. Then she slipped her hand lower. "What about this spot? Is it fixed, too?"

"Not quite."

"Does what I'm doing help any?"

"Only if you keep doing it."

She kept on and on. Rafe closed his eyes and let her wield her womanly power. She was the woman of his dreams, and he was a fool for her. He knew he'd be a sad, lonely fool after she returned to San Francisco in less than a week.

He'd be a dead fool after that, if his plan didn't work. Not that he could think much past the present moment with Terra in bed beside him doing wondrous things with her soft, supple hand.

So he closed his eyes and stopped thinking. He was a fool in love.

TERRA CRAMMED a lot of work into the next morning, including her daily call to Macy.

Macy was jubilant. "Ta da! We're going to be in the news."

"What news?"

"The *Chronicle* food section. A reporter dropped in this morning, doing a feature article on menu writers, so I wasted no time telling her how fantastic Camden Consulting is. She boggled when I said you were at Bride's Bay doing big things there. She's going to lead off her piece with us."

"You better have told her you're my assistant, not my secretary, Macy Medford."

"Actually, I did, but it scared me half to death to say it."

"You're finally accepting my offer after more than a week of waffling about it?"

"If you'll still have me once you see my practice projects, yes."

"Congratulations!" Terra exclaimed. "Run a help-wanted ad for your replacement!"

"Don't you want to see my projects first?"

"Of course not. They were just to keep you from having a nervous breakdown while I'm gone." Terra bit her lip, not wanting to think of how little time was left, yet needing to face it.

Macy said, "It's a good thing you're coming back soon because there's more superb news. Bradford

Congden called ten minutes ago and wants you for all four of his South Bay restaurants."

"Wants *us*, Macy. Superb is the word. You'll be just the help I need."

"Good thing you got a vacation tucked into your project there. After the news feature, we're going to be even hotter than we are, I'll bet. Still having fun there?"

"Hours and hours." Terra's hormones sent up a heat wave in memory of the reckless, perilous hours she'd spent with Rafe. There would be more later today, after she finished taking a boat lesson.

"Have you stolen Kent away from me yet?"

"No, and neither has anyone else. He's all yours to daydream about."

"Really, you haven't even had a teensy romance?"

"No teensy anything." Only an enormously dangerous, nerve-racking affair.

They concluded the call and Terra returned to work with Columbia in the main kitchen. Though busy and productive, Terra found herself so impatient to be with Rafe again that the time seemed to crawl.

Impatient, impetuous, swept away by emotions and a situation she couldn't control, she hardly knew herself. She knew one thing, though: she'd never be the same Terra Camden after this.

TIME MOVED AN IOTA faster that afternoon when Terra learned the basics of motorboating with one of Kent's marina assistants, Bobby Boyes, a likable twenty-one-year-old. Kent himself was attending one of Thomas Graves's security procedures classes. Terra had heard complaints in the employee ranks about the manda-

tory classes, and the extensive surveillance system he
was designing for the resort.

Bobby, a bit cocky and quite voluble, grumbled, too,
as he gave her motorboating advice in a small inboard
model. "This place is going to be so tight-laced," he
complained. "Wherever you turn there'll be a security
camera staring you in the eye. Half of the time nobody
will know if they're being watched or not. It gives me
the creeps."

"Management must feel it's necessary," Terra reasoned, steering figure eights in the bay at his direction
with an ease and enjoyment that surprised her.

"True," Bobby conceded reluctantly, "some weird
things have happened around here before now. Even a
murder back in March, which nobody likes mentioned."

"There was a small item in the San Francisco pa-
pers," Terra recalled.

"It was mondo news in S.C.," Bobby said, rolling his
eyes. "Not as bad publicity as Miz Elizabeth's grandson, but not good, however you cut it."

Terra kept a neutral expression. "Rafe Jermain, you
mean? Liz's brother?"

Bobby nodded. "*That's* as bad as anything gets. Not
that I'd ever say so around the Jermain family. I was a
kid when that happened and from then to now there's
never been a word out of the Jermains about him except 'no comment.'"

Terra shivered inside, thinking of the news flash there
would be about Rafe now should he come to light. She
had a sinking suspicion that the undisclosed part of
Rafe's plan had something to do with the upcoming

diplomats' conference. If he intended to enter the hotel property in a bid to prove something, hidden cameras would catch him on film.

She wished she could pump the employees she knew best about the conference without them wondering why and perhaps reporting it to the security chief. But since it was unrelated to her work, they'd wonder. What would a menu specialist care about a conference that would occur after she left Bride's Bay? Why would she want to know if there were any Leons on the conference list?

How could she find out? Perhaps by a simple call to the future bookings line to confirm whether he had a reservation or not. She resolved to make that call, from a pay phone rather than her room, so no one would know who was curious.

"You know," Bobby said, "you're taking to this boat like a champ. You're ready to try a spin around the island."

During that spin, Bobby explained about tide schedules. At just the right point, she oh-so-innocently got him to show her how to pull up at the Hamiltons' pier and cast on in case she ever wanted to "stop by and see Lalie" while boating. It scared her how good she was getting at criminal conspiracy.

She was even shrewd enough to say blithely, "Hmm, I might even rent this little charm one evening and cruise around Charleston, see the city lights."

"You bet," Bobby agreed. "Guests do it all the time on nice nights. Some put in there for the nightlife. Bride's Bay is a snooze after dark compared to

Charleston and, hey, the last ferry to here is at midnight. Way too early, for sure, when you're having fun."

Although she didn't need to know where to dock in Charleston, she asked anyway, since it seemed a likely question for an out-of-town boater to ask.

"The marina where we dock the *Indigo Moon*," he said. "With clear weather and a compass, back and forth from here to there is a snap."

All very comforting to know. All for an illegal purpose. Rafe hadn't revealed exactly why he wanted to go to Charleston, but she was certain it wouldn't comfort her to know. She was afraid he wanted to get a gun there, by hook or by crook. Either way could get him caught.

As for the Leon angle, she called future bookings from the marina pay phone after she finished with Bobby. The reservations clerk searched the conference reservations for first-or last-named Leons and found none.

Rafe's intentions remained a mystery.

RAFE REFUSED TO ANSWER her questions later, when she went to him after her boat session. She went, of course, because there was no staying away now, because he was her lover and she was too much in love with him to stop herself.

He cut off her inquiries with hot, heady kisses that sent the questions melting to the back of her mind.

"Rafe, you're not answering m—"

His tongue slid in against hers, not a reply, but a sensual request for her undivided attention to his need for her. It was insatiable, urgent, unquenchable—like her own need for him.

His mouth eating hers, he unbuttoned her blouse enough for her breasts to spill out into his hands. Thumbs focused on the taut tips, he circled and pressed, circled and pressed.

Terra's mind hazed with desire, losing recall of whatever questions she'd had. She slid her hands under his shirt and then went to the bed without question, desire exploding within her, hunger so explicit and primitive that she was gasping from it before they even got their clothes off.

Rafe's caresses were urgent as she sank down to sit on the edge of the bed. He knelt on one knee at the side of it, his hips framed by her legs, and suckled her breasts, sending shock waves radiating from the sensitive peaks to the throbbing ache between her thighs.

His tongue swirled on her, curled around her nipples, side to side, left them hot and wet when his mouth drew away to kiss her shoulders and the valley between her breasts.

"Terra," he breathed, "Terra."

She framed his face in her hands, thinking, *I love you, Rafe. I always will, no matter what*. But she didn't speak the words to him, knowing instinctively that her emotions would only add to his heavy burden of danger and uncertainty.

She simply invited more kisses and caresses from him, stroking his hair as his head moved lower, as his hands pushed up her skirt.

Then he was the one gasping loudly, for she had come to him bare and welcoming, eager for him, wearing nothing under the skirt. So eager.

He muttered something dark and impetuous as she leaned back slightly, parting her thighs a fraction wider for him to take his pleasure and give to hers.

"For you, Rafe," she murmured. "Only you."

"The luckiest man in the world," he rejoined huskily, stroking his fingers from her knees inward along the tender surface of her inner thighs, then brushing his fingertips lightly over the curly cloud of hair that shielded her secrets. "I can't tell you how beautiful you are. You've just got to take my word."

He kissed the path his fingers had taken, each side, drawing his open lips along her skin until she was writhing for him to do more, more.

He did, nuzzling her downy center, tasting within, laving her sultry folds with his tongue and then capturing her tenderest flesh between his lips.

Terra laced her fingers in his hair and reveled in the emotion, the sensation, the exquisite intimacy of his loving mouth. She responded, willing and trusting, panting with pleasure.

"Oh, Rafe . . . yes . . . please . . ."

Her fingers clenched, her hips tensed, lifted up and up to the crest and beyond. His name burst from her in a broken chant as she released to him without reserve, lost to the depths of her heart in love.

LATER, THEY DRIFTED, their bodies loose and languid as they lay together under the moon-starred fresco, Rafe on his back and she on her side next to him.

"Rafe, one question."

He stopped sifting her hair through his fingers. "Don't ask again. For your own good, I'm not going to tell you."

"It's not about your plan."

"Oh." He took up sifting again. "What?"

"Did you have any serious relationships before?"

"Nothing serious." He was silent a moment. "There was someone special, though. But it was a long time ago, and prison did some strange things to my memories of her. And strange things to the rest of me, too."

Terra didn't like wanting to know what she wanted to know. But she couldn't help probing. "What was she like?

"You don't want to know about her, okay?"

"You still care about her, then."

"I don't kiss and tell, Terra. Would you tell me about the lovers you've had?"

"Ah, so you were lovers."

"Terra, for Pete's sake, what is this with you all of a sudden?"

"It's curiosity of the ugliest sort," she agreed ruefully. "Why, I can't say. Jealousy, maybe, or a competitive streak I didn't know I had until right now. I'm sorry, truly I am."

Rafe gave her a slow, forgiving smile. "I'm not such a saint myself, to be honest. I've wondered more than a few times about your love life in San Francisco."

"It's best described as few and far between," she told him frankly. "I don't have any talent for serial relationships."

"Well, if you're still curious—and don't take it the wrong way—you remind me a little of my memorable lover. At any rate, it was a unique situation and she called herself Mermaid. So there, you know."

Soft tears sprang to Terra's eyes and a tremulous smile quivered her lips. "Ohhh, how romantic."

Rafe turned her face to his and pressed a soft kiss to her lips. "You're what's romantic. And beautiful, understanding, smart, sexy—"

Terra stopped him with a kiss, tender and true from her heart to his. Mermaid, mother of his son. Later, alone, she'd cry bittersweet tears for the unknowing gift her child's father had given her.

THE NEXT AFTERNOON, Terra took a boat out by herself after another session with Bobby. She put the boat in at the Hamiltons' pier, the tide being right for it, and went to Lalie's to get Josh.

The day before, Rafe had asked her to bring the boy for another swim. "I miss the little guy," Rafe had said somewhat wistfully. Heartwarmed by his request, Terra had agreed.

They had a wonderful time that afternoon, the three of them together in the pool. It was well worth foregoing the sexual intimacy she could otherwise have had with Rafe during that precious time, and she loved him all the more for not wanting only sex with her.

At the same time, though, she was tortured by thoughts of Josh's reaction should Rafe get captured. It would be news she'd have a tough time keeping from a child Josh's age. TV, newspapers, magazines would show Rafe's face, and how would she prevent Josh from seeing every image? Would Josh be convinced that Kermit and Rafe Jermain looked a lot alike, but weren't the same man?

Kermit. Thank heaven—Lalie—at least, for that whimsical name.

Watching father and son play in the pool, Terra was acutely aware of precious time passing too quickly. Only a few more days remained before she'd leave Bride's Bay and never see Rafe again. Unless his plan worked, whatever it was. If it didn't, what then? He was taking the boat to Charleston tonight. Why?

She wanted to know! And she wasn't the only one. Lalie was fretting about it, too. But Rafe wasn't saying a word.

TERRA TOOK THE BOAT back to the marina after leaving the estate late in the afternoon. Josh loved the ride, of course, everything about it. Back at the marina, she rented the boat in advance for the evening and later had dinner with Josh in the employee cafeteria. After that, Lalie came by and collected Josh to baby-sit him at her own house.

With Josh taken care of, Terra dressed as if casual dance clubs might be on her evening agenda and took a warm coat along with her to the boat. Kent was in the marina office when she got there and, to her alarm, the security chief, Thomas Graves, was also present.

They both seemed more concerned than Bobby had been about her plan to cruise around Charleston on her own. Graves, a no-nonsense man in his early fifties, had hawklike blue eyes and an unobtrusive manner that

Lalie had mentioned was deceptive. Terra was instantly on guard, although careful not to show it.

She kept a confident, mildly surprised expression, as she countered their concern. "I understand it's not unusual for guests to boat to Charleston. You feel I'll have more problems than other guests do after several hours of boating lessons?"

"Not very many guests go to Charleston alone," Kent patiently explained.

"Single females, you mean?" she asked not quite innocently. "Or single guests in general?" She met each man's eyes with an engaging, inquiring smile that found it impossible to believe a nice, world-class resort would discriminate against anyone's gender.

Kent and Graves exchanged discomfited glances. Graves said, "Point well taken, Ms. Camden. Still, be sure to stay on course between ports, and if you debark in Charleston, take care."

"I appreciate your understandable concern," she said graciously, "but rest assured that a native San Franciscan like me has plenty of day-to-day, big-city experience."

They both looked as if they'd made a regrettable judgment call, if not an outright blunder, so she gave them a forgiving smile and put out her hand for the key.

"Anything else before I go?"

In nervous, embarrassed unison, they both replied, "No, ma'am."

Kent hastened to give her the key and offered his help to get her started and on her way. She accepted gladly, as if she found limited chivalry agreeable at times, and Graves bowed out in a controlled hurry.

Going to the boat with Kent, Terra was amazed at how *very* good she'd gotten in the art of deception and criminal conspiracy. Daunting the estimable security chief was no easy task, yet he'd practically scuffed his toes on the floorboards with sorry-ma'am chagrin.

"You've got a nice night for an outing," Kent commented idly while she put on a life vest. "Warm, clear, full moon."

"Perfect," she agreed, taking a deep, appreciative breath of the evening air. Then, as if a thought had just that minute occurred to her, she said, "You know, I think I'll buzz around the island a time or two before I head to the mainland."

There was the possibility that Kent or anyone else might watch her progress out of the bay and wonder when she turned north rather than continuing due east. Circling the island explained everything in advance.

"It's sure the right night for it with the moon and all," Kent said. "A lot of boats are out all around, so keep a sharp eye. Have a good one."

"See you later, Kent. Much later, no doubt." She turned the key in the ignition, he cast off her line and she backed out of the slip.

With a seemingly carefree wave, she was on her way, only a minute or so later than she had planned. All her bases were covered, thank heaven, and Rafe was waiting for her.

11

RAFE WAS WEARING dark, casual clothing from the
Hamiltons' enormous wardrobe when Terra got to the
estate. He had a wool beret to cover his hair, and sunglasses to conceal his eyes. There was also a telescop-
ing white cane which Lalie had mail-ordered for him.
Without the cane, he brought to mind a rather pros-
perous jazz musician, visually impaired.

"What do you think?" he asked.

"I'm afraid you'll attract more attention as a blind
man than not," she decided.

He shook his head. "It's not human nature for seeing
people to stare at the blind. Handicaps make unim-
paired people uncomfortable, so they avoid looking."

Terra couldn't recall ever taking keen notice of anyone with a white cane. What Rafe said was true, at least
in her own case. She hoped he was right about others.

"You'll see," he said. Retracting the cane to a twelve-
inch length, he tucked it into his sleeve along his forearm and hooked the glasses over the ribbed neck of his
sweater. "I'll be blind when it suits my purpose, and not
blind when it doesn't."

"What purpose?"

He refused to answer. "Just give me the boat key."

"Rafe, anything could happen to you. Your spine is
still injured and so is your knee. They could give out,

the fever could hit you—what would you do in an emergency?"

"There aren't going to be any emergencies. I know what I'm doing. It won't take long."

"To do what?"

"Give me the key."

"If something unexpected happens to you, and you don't come back, what about the boat?"

He shrugged. "Apparently someone, a hot-wire artist, stole it when you came back to Lalie's to get Josh. This house wouldn't have a security system if all people were honest, you know. Boat theft occurs and it could happen to you, maybe tonight."

"Answer what happens if you come down with fever in Charleston."

"That's a chance I have to take." He put out his hand for the key.

Terra didn't comply. She picked up the phone and dialed Lalie. "Hi, Terra here. If you can keep Josh, I'm going with Rafe. Yes, maybe late. I know. Thanks a million." She hung up.

Rafe stared at her. "Like hell you're going with me."

"I've got the key," she said, "you want the boat, figure it out."

"No way." He shook his head. "If I get into hot water and you get burned—nope, uh-uh."

Terra pulled out the waistband of her stretch leggings and dropped the key inside. She wiggled it down to a secure, private area and let the snug band snap back. Then, folding her arms in front of her, she tapped her toe impatiently.

"You heard me, Rafe."

He clenched his fists. "You're in danger enough as it is. Do you want to leave Josh an orphan?"

She retorted, "What are you planning to do in Charleston that's so dangerous to human life?"

"Things happen, Terra. Like the soccer ball, last thing anyone would expect. I don't want things happening to you, or to Josh by extension. Me, fine. Not you two."

"Maybe you mean to fly the coop tonight and that's why you want to go alone. Maybe you *are* guilty and have no intention of proving otherwise."

Rafe's tone turned to ice. "I may be unable to prove it to anyone's satisfaction when the time comes, but I'll give it the only try I've got."

"Time is wasting," Terra advised, tapping her toe. "Make up your mind."

Rafe stepped up to her and gripped her shoulders. "You know what's wrong with you, Terra?"

"Only one thing, Rafe." She wrenched herself out of his hold. "I love you!"

For a long moment he looked stunned, confused. Then he growled, "Love, hell! You don't even trust me to come back tonight."

"It may not be up to you whether you come back. If that happens, you'll need help."

"Not yours, Terra."

"You're guilty, then. Is that it? I love a guilty man who's on his way out of here for good?"

"No." His expression took on a look of anguish and he came to her swiftly, capturing her in his arms. "Jesus, Terra, what do you mean 'love'?"

Although incensed beyond all patience with him, she yielded to his embrace nevertheless. Sharp tears stung her eyes and her voice broke. "It's not what I want or intended. It just . . . happened."

He gave a soft curse, held her tight, rubbing his chin on the crown of her head. "It makes everything that much worse, you know."

"Tell me about it," she scoffed thickly, burrowing her face against his chest, trembling with anger and love and fear.

Cheek upon his heart, Terra felt the vibrant beat, the precious seconds of life it measured. His future was a question with no discernable answer, his existence tenuous and provisional, up in the air.

Rafe's arms wrapped even more tightly around her. "Believe me, I *can* tell you about it. I love you, too."

"Oh, Rafe. You do?" She sagged against him. "Just what we need."

"Yeah. The last thing in the world."

He nudged her face up to his and kissed her with deep, emotional intensity. Against her lips, he protested, "It shouldn't be like this, not something we both regret. But there it is, regrets all around."

"I'm going with you, Rafe."

He gave a gritty, prolonged and finally relenting sigh. "Okay. But do whatever I say from now on until we get back here. Whether it makes sense to you or not. Promise me that."

"I promise."

"Good, I'll hold you to it." He kissed her once more, then slowly released her as if there might not be a next time for them. "How about that key now?"

"You can retrieve it yourself," she replied agreeably, "in the boat."

"For a softhearted woman," he murmured, brushing his knuckles where the key rested at the base of her pelvis, "you drive a hard bargain. You know that?"

She caught her breath at his magic touch. "With you, I have to. Let's go."

CHARLESTON HARBOR WAS impressive, illuminated by the full moon and city lights. At the wheel of the boat, Rafe steered into the Cooper River and put into what Terra felt sure was the equivalent of an unmarked, illegal parking space on the east side of Charleston at one of the wharves.

"No one will ticket us here," he said, adding that he knew his tricks in the waters around the city. "Trust me."

Terra did; she had to. The spot was dark, cramped, obscure, but accessible. The adjacent area was a construction site, in a state of upheaval.

They got out and picked their way through the rubble to a dank, narrow alley where she saw several derelicts asleep in dustbins. Rafe put on the sunglasses and took out the cane.

"A blind dude and a babe, out for a stroll," he said with a grim chuckle, linking arms with her and then sweeping the stick in front of him as they moved down the alley.

She told him, "You should have grown a beard to conceal more."

"I decided against it because it's too much of a marker and hard to get rid of if I need to. Shaving off a heavy beard while on the run takes time, a place, razor, water."

"I never thought of it that way."

"You're not a desperate fugitive."

"I've begun thinking like one, though." She told him about the security chief and the fast talking she'd done. "Me, Terra Camden, unbelievable."

"Have a quick thought right now," Rafe muttered. "Look who's coming."

Terra gulped, seeing two policemen on foot turn into the alley from the cross street ahead of them. "What if they ask why we're here?"

"Keep cool. Walk on by as if we belong."

Terra thought the cops already looked suspicious as they approached. She broke her promise to Rafe immediately and spoke to them. "Help, we've gotten lost."

Rafe's arm, linked with hers, tensed steel hard as the officers approached and stopped.

"We've gotten all turned around, I'm afraid," she told them with smiling confusion. "We're looking for, um," she blinked at Rafe wide-eyed, "what's the name of it, darling?"

He growled the name of, surprisingly, a toy store.

"For our son's birthday present," she added to that. "Or is the store closed this evening?"

The officers relaxed and assured them the store was open until ten. They gave careful directions, then wished a happy day to the birthday boy.

"Andrew," Terra told them proudly. "Four years old, going on five. Thank you so much for setting us right."

"No problem, ma'am," the cops assured her and continued on their way, presumably to roust the transients out of the bins.

"There," Terra said to Rafe as she moved on with him. "They couldn't be less suspicious."

"I've only got a heart attack to recover from," Rafe muttered. "You promised you'd do as I say."

"I didn't know we'd run into cops in a dark, sleazy alley."

"Well, quit improvising unless I tell you to. This is my life on the line here."

"It's our love on the line, as well," she countered. "Although, if you ever get cleared of crime, you're bound to take up your old sea-roving life and forget about me. I don't know why I'm doing anything for you when all you want to do is give me orders."

He said testily, "The peace and quiet of my old life would be a plus at the moment. Chatty Cathy isn't my idea of the perfect accomplice."

"You're stuck with imperfect me. Too nervous to shut up after running into cops right away."

"I've got half a mind to send you back on the ferry."

"As if I'd follow that order any better."

"You promised."

"I take it back."

They were out of the alley and on the city sidewalks now, for some reason following the cops' directions. Rafe switched his white stick from side to side with fractious vigor. The presence of passersby forced them to keep their voices low.

"If I ever did get cleared of charges, I sure as hell would go back to roving the sea. Arguing with you every ten minutes would drive me to it."

Terra gritted her teeth, certain that any love she'd had for Rafe Jermain was a thing of the past. "Where are we going, anyway?"

"First to a hotel that does big banquet business. Then we'll stop at the toy store."

"Toy store? What for?"

"I want to get Josh something."

Terra was too taken aback—and too touched—to say another word. She debated with herself whether she should ever tell Rafe about Josh. No. At least, not yet.

"Why are we going to a hotel?"

"Don't ask."

"Couldn't you give me a harmless hint?"

"I'm going to rent a room and ravish you there all night."

She missed a step. "You aren't."

"No, but I'd love to." He glanced around, tense and wary, yet appreciative of being out in the open and able to move freely. He could almost pretend that he was free, out for a night with his sweetheart.

"All right, I'll stop asking questions," Terra grumbled. "Any special orders for me before we get to the hotel?"

"Sit in the lobby, read a magazine while I'm busy elsewhere in the building, and *do not* move."

They walked a few blocks from the toy store to a big, busy hotel. Rafe stopped at the bulletin board and stood there as if Terra were the one reading the schedule of events taking place there that day. There were four banquets, a wedding reception, two meetings of insurance underwriters and other assorted affairs.

Seeing just what he needed, he left her in a chair in the lobby and went up to the mezzanine in an elevator.

Once there, a blind man searching for the right event among several being held on that floor, he came to the one that had the best chance of aiding his plan. A noisy dinner for some three hundred diners, many of them milling around in the room.

He entered, made a quick visual scan and then wended his way with his stick around the perimeter of the room. At one point, the most critical, he deliberately collided with a waiter who was bearing a full tray of bread baskets and tripped the man with his cane.

Not an accident, of course, though it looked like one. The waiter stumbled and sprawled to the floor, tray and dinner rolls bouncing around him.

"Oh, wow, sorry," Rafe said, pretending to feel around in order to find the poor guy and help him up out of the crumbs. The waiter's captain rushed over to help.

After the waiter got righted, with all the fumbling assistance that Rafe could offer, the commotion died down and Rafe was informed that no, this was not the wedding reception he said he was seeking.

The captain helpfully oriented him to the door and Rafe returned to the elevator for the short ride down to the lobby. There, he bumbled into the men's room, turned his reversible sweater inside out to a light gray, tossed his beret in the waste bin, and hid his cane in his sleeve again. He had to keep the glasses on, though, and hope people would assume he had extremely light-sensitive eyes.

Finally, he took what he needed from the poor guy's wallet, and then turned it in to the shoe-shine man as something someone had apparently lost.

That much accomplished, he went to Terra, who blinked at the change in his clothes.

"Let's get out of here," he said, and hurried her out of the hotel.

12

IN FRONT OF the toy store, Rafe said, "Don't argue about coming inside. Security cameras would pick us up together, and if someone there sees through me you'd get fingered, too. Wait across the street at the bus stop so it won't look as if you're loitering."

"Rafe, why endanger yourself just to buy Josh something?"

"Don't ask."

"I have a right to some answers, Rafe. You're not in this alone, you know."

"Keep your voice down, and for Pete's sake don't call me by name again."

Terra went coldly silent, did as he said and crossed the street. Traffic was busy, buses arrived and departed. After a while, it seemed to her that Rafe was taking a little too long to buy a toy.

Tense and nervous, she shifted from one foot to the other, back and forth, trying to assure herself that he was gone so long because the store was big.

She had paralyzing thoughts of a store clerk detecting that he was Rafe Jermain behind the dark glasses. The fluorescents inside looked bright, as if they'd turn up every detail. Would an unsuspecting clerk detect who he was, even though everyone thought him dead?

Terra squeezed her eyes shut. It was frightening how much she loved him. Suddenly, an awful thought struck her. *What if there's a back way out of the store and he took it? Gave me the slip? He has the key to the boat!*

Dismayed by the thought, she sucked in a breath so loudly that everyone at the bus stop turned and stared at her. Then they all turned away, distracted by the approach of a bus.

Terra backed up to the bank building behind her, needing solid support, and tried not to hyperventilate. Tried to think what she'd do. She'd have to take the ferry back to the island. Did she have enough money for the fare? But first, before anything, she'd have to report the boat stolen and somehow explain why she'd left it in that cranny by the construction site.

Oh, damn, it was all too unexplainable and convoluted. Had Rafe played her for a complete fool? It was beginning to look like it. The longer she stood there the more certain she felt.

Terra pressed her hand against her mouth to stifle another dismayed gasp. *Idiot!*

RAFE STEPPED OUT of the toy store and glimpsed Terra across the street. She had her head down, one arm folded at her waist, the other elbow propped on the folded arm and her hand over her eyes. Was she crying? Feeling ill?

A bus suddenly blocked his view of her as he hastened to the pedestrian crosswalk and waited with other pedestrians for the light to change. One woman gave him an odd look, probably because of his sunglasses, but he didn't react.

Unfortunately, she waddled at a snail's pace in front of him during the cross on the green light. He reached the other curb and his heart sank when he saw past the bus. Terra was gone.

Gripping his bag from the store, he turned slowly on the corner, looking around for her. Disappeared. Just like that. He scanned the bus windows for her face, thinking she might have gotten on for some inexplicable reason. No Terra on board.

Then it came to him that maybe she'd gotten so ticked about the answers he hadn't given her that she'd decided to go back on the ferry. Whatever, she wasn't where he'd left her. She'd said she loved him, but now she was gone.

For all he knew, she might be chasing down the cops to arrest him.

He didn't know what else to think. Maybe she *had* changed her mind about everything and decided the danger wasn't worth it. At any rate, not knowing where she was, he decided the boat would be a stupid place to go.

He moved down the sidewalk, growing increasingly certain that Terra had come to the end of her involvement in the conspiracy.

Love, hell, he started to think. *What kind of fool have I been?*

He came to the end of the block, turned the corner and walked straight into Terra.

"Jeez," he breathed, so relieved to see her he felt dizzy. "What are you— Why are you—"

Looking drenched with relief to see him, she gestured at an automatic teller machine built into the side of the bank building. "I needed some cash." She drew a deep breath. "What took you so long?"

"I got it gift-wrapped," he said, gesturing with the bag. "The clerk took forever."

It wasn't entirely the truth, but he wasn't going to tell her what he'd done all that time. She didn't need to know he'd met with a sleazy lowlife in the back alley who had access to security clearances for hotel employees.

"What next?" Terra asked.

"Not a thing," he assured her.

They hastened to the boat and returned to Jermain's Island without further incident. There, Terra got Josh from Lalie's and left to return the boat.

"HEY," KENT SAID with surprise when she and Josh arrived at the marina. "Calling it an early night?" He checked his watch. "It's 11:00 p.m."

"I guess I'm just not the club hopper I used to be," Terra said. She tousled Josh's hair. "I went shopping for Josh instead."

Josh had Rafe's gift to him, the Power Ranger set, clutched in his arms like a priceless treasure.

Kent admired Josh's present, then said to her, "The word going around is your menus are fabulous, to quote Miz Elizabeth. Your job is almost done, I've heard."

Terra nodded. "Three more days to completion. Home again for us, right, Josh?"

"I wanna stay here," Josh informed them stoutly, his eyes a little sleepy from being awakened to leave Lalie's.

Kent chuckled. "You'd blend right in with the Jermains, that's for sure. Miz Elizabeth and Liz are still shaking their heads about you."

Terra was shaking hers, too, because no one had made any more than a marveling matter of Josh's Jermain traits. She left the marina and went to her room with Josh, exhausted. In love. Confused. Fearful.

And depressed about everything ending so soon.

TERRA HADN'T KNOWN three days could pass as swiftly as her last ones at Bride's Bay did. Each one was full to bursting with work, time with Josh, time with Rafe and never enough time with both of them together.

On the last day, she spent late in the afternoon and into the early evening alone with Rafe. In his arms, after making love under the fresco, she sighed and held back her tears.

"What's going to happen to you, Rafe?"

"Who knows? The Hamiltons come back in three weeks, so that's it for my hideout. None of the estates stay in mothballs through the summer months, so I'll have to look elsewhere. Maybe South America if I can make it to there."

"You've abandoned your plan to prove yourself, then."

He shrugged. "Could be."

"Don't ask, in other words. Not about that or Leon or anything else."

"Stay innocent of me after you leave here, Terra. For your own sake and Josh's. And my peace of mind."

"Rafe, if somehow you prove yourself, what would it mean for us?"

He shook his head. "No matter what happens, you'll have a lot more decent life without me. One thing about being accused of a crime is that the taint lingers even when innocence is proven.

"I don't see myself with a wife and stepchild whose lives would be shadowed by who I am. So go back to San Francisco," he said gently, "find some nice, clean guy to love. One that Josh can be proud to call Daddy. Somebody people don't speculate and whisper about whether he lives one more day or a hundred years."

Terra framed his face in her hands. "You may be the only man for me, Rafe."

"Don't, Terra. Don't make me guilty of that. And please, please don't cry."

"Make love to me again. Maybe I won't be able to do that and cry at the same time."

She gave herself to Rafe for the last time and he took her with intense, loving care, making the final shared moments last and last. And before it was over, Terra did cry despite Rafe's plea. He kissed her tears away, but really there was no telling whose tears were whose at the very end.

It was goodbye. "Our way," Terra whispered in heartbroken farewell.

THE NEXT DAY, she and Josh boarded the *Indigo Moon* for the first leg of their trip home. She was surprised and pleased when several Bride's Bay people turned out at the dock. Columbia and Lalie, of course, and Shad, Joanie, Elise, Caitlin, Bobby.

Miz Elizabeth and Judge Bradshaw were there, but not Liz who had done a mysterious disappearing act again. Joanie had promised to send Terra a news flash if anyone ever discovered where Liz went, and with whom. Even Thomas Graves strolled out and offered his good wishes.

Waving goodbye, Terra blew a kiss over their heads to the estate where Rafe was hidden. Good or bad, guilty or innocent, the only man for her.

BACK IN SAN FRANCISCO, Terra did her best to return Rafe to her past. She immersed herself in the four-restaurant deal with Bradford Congden. Work was coming in left and right after the *Chronicle* feature article.

It put Macy in a tizzy of self-doubt about whether she could be the strong right arm Terra needed. Terra set her the task of interviewing the applicants for the secretarial position so that Macy would soon free up to be all she could be.

The return to normal life was consuming and demanding. Terra had to squeeze in time to catch up with her parents and watch the videos of their Mexico trip. Josh's preschool had an open house, another chunk of time.

Underneath everything, she worried about Rafe, missed him, longed for him. Each night when Josh blessed Kermit in his bedtime prayers, she almost broke down.

Against Rafe's wishes, Lalie had promised to call if anything happened with him. So far, no call. Maybe Rafe had convinced Lalie not to. Terra wrote a letter, but only with news of herself and Josh, no mention of Rafe. Lalie wrote back in much the same vein.

Each morning when Terra rushed through reading the newspaper, she kept an eye out for news of the Caribbean diplomats' conference and the President's vacation. There were a few news items about the conference and the notable dignitaries who were to attend. The Haitian, Clovis Lecours, got most of the coverage. Brief mentions went to Jacquies Noel-Cooke from Montinerro and Puerto Rico's Javier Delgado.

Terra smiled a little, thinking of the menus they would all consult for their meals, from breakfast to banquet. Her own creative design and copy combined with Columbia's brilliant cuisine—they could both be proud.

Now Terra had another celebrity chef to please, Bradford Congden of San Francisco fame. She could do Brad proud. And she would. Just as she had done for Columbia Hanes.

ON THE FRIDAY NIGHT of her first week back, Terra left work and stopped by her parents' house to get Josh. Her father was watching the evening news when she came in.

"Bride's Bay on the tube," he said.

Watching with him, she learned that the President's vacation there was semiofficial. Thomas Graves was shown for a few seconds, affirming that Bride's Bay security would be more than equal to protecting the First Couple.

Terra's dad patted her shoulder and spoke to the TV screen. "My sweetpea did the menus there, Mr. President and Ms. First Lady. Three cheers for her!"

The reporter marveled at how the resort had survived the political bombshell of Rafe Jermain's treachery and continued with its sterling reputation intact. The news piece went on about the diplomats' conference.

It would begin the next night, with speeches from three of the many key players: Haiti, Montinerro, Puerto Rico. Lecours and Delgado were pictured arriving in the resort's helicopter. The Montinerran arrived on a yacht named after himself.

Describing America's now-close ties with Montinerro, once a despised enemy, the reporter marveled, "How times have changed in five years. Today, Rafe Jermain could supply all the arms he'd like to Montinerro without even bruising a law, much less breaking one."

There was another shot of the Montinerran yacht docking in grand style at the marina. Terra thought she recognized Kent on the dock. Then something else caught her eye and held it. The yacht's name, *Noel-Cooke*, isolated on the hull.

Suddenly she saw something she hadn't seen about that name until that very moment, something the average person wouldn't notice but a word-crafter might.

She pulled in a loud, sharp gasp. "That's it!

"What?" Her dad stared at her.

She put a trembling hand to her forehead. "I've got to go back there. Right away."

"Back? Why?"

"Leon."

"Who?"

"Noel spelled backward!"

IT TOOK TERRA all day Saturday to fly from San Francisco to Charleston on short notice, and she got there at five that afternoon by zigzagging across the country on the only flights she could get.

Her parents, still wondering what on earth was the matter with her, had Josh at their house for the weekend. She had left them hanging as to when she'd be back.

Lalie met her at the Charleston airport, looking drawn and worried. "Rafe is gone," she said, tears standing in her eyes. "Without a trace, or a word to me."

"What? Since when?"

"Since sometime before you called me, I figure. I phoned him right after your call, to tell him you were coming, and no answer. The house is empty. No sign that he was ever there. Everything spic and span, just the way the Hamiltons left it."

"Oh, no." Terra hadn't foreseen this. Rafe gone.

They sat down in the terminal.

"Why have you come back here, Terra?"

"I'm not sure, Lalie. Even if I knew for certain, it might be best for you not to know."

"You sound like Rafe saying the less *everybody* knows, the better. Lord, I miss that boy. I'm so afraid he's dead somewhere. Or sick to death with chills and fever."

"Oh, Lalie, don't even think it. Please. If you lose faith, how am I going to have any?" Terra tried to keep calm and be rational. "Rafe gave no clue that he was leaving?"

"Not one. He was the same as always when I took dinner to him last night. Well, not the same, but he hasn't been himself since you left. Very subdued since then."

"You didn't see him after that?"

"No. Then you called early this morning and I called him and here we are." Lalie dabbed her eyes with a tissue. "How's that little Josh you left behind?"

"Fine. He blesses you every night in his prayers." Terra's throat swelled. "And Kermit, too."

"Well, we all need blessings right now, that is for certain. Let's get ourselves up and on our way home. I'm so glad to have company again, since Josh left a big hole."

They took a cab to the ferry and during the ferry ride Terra revealed her hunch that Rafe's plan had to do with the conference and the Montinerran diplomat.

She sighed. "If he still has a plan and hasn't flown the coop. I don't know, Lalie. Maybe I'm just overimaginative, putting one and one together and coming up with the wrong sum."

"You got the right sum when you and Rafe put one and one together. Falling in love as you did, that just added up the way things should."

Terra nodded. "If things could ever work out, Rafe is the only man for me."

"What do you plan to do now that you're here?"

"I want to see the keynote speeches tonight. They'll be televised, I understand, but I'd like to be there. Maybe Columbia could get me in?"

"*Us* in," Lalie corrected. "If something's going to go down tonight, I want to be there."

"Nothing may happen, as well."

"You've got a strong intuition, though," Lalie stated. "It led you this far and still hasn't stopped."

"If Rafe is gone, though," Terra mused with tears threatening, "none of it matters. But if he isn't gone and something terrible happens . . ." She trailed off miserably.

Lalie went to the phone. "I'll call Columbia. She'll get us in or my name isn't Hanes."

COLUMBIA DID GET THEM IN, at a small table with Miz Elizabeth and Judge Bradshaw. The couple had not wanted to make tedious small talk with strangers that evening at the banquet, but welcomed a family friend and Terra to dine with them and hear the keynote addresses.

They were naturally surprised that Terra had returned so soon. She waved it off, saying she'd had a bit of business to do in Charleston. "Branching out," she said, and they thought that just dandy.

Security was high for the occasion, with everyone's attendance badges checked at the banquet hall door. The media people all wore press badges, and the serving staff had their own union IDs.

Dinner was served, with Terra too nervous to pay more than scant attention to what was set before her. A soup, a main course, a sorbet, dessert. The banquet hall, too, might have been a horse stable for all it mattered to her. Under the table, she pleated and unpleated her napkin with tense, clammy fingers.

Finally, the speeches began, with a change from the printed program that put Jacquies Noel-Cooke first. A suave, handsome man in his mid-forties, he had a deep suntan and an engaging manner.

He spoke at length, words which Terra never quite registered because she kept thinking of what Rafe had said about Leon. If Noel-Cooke was the same person, and Terra felt certain he was, he was a treacherous man, a murderous opportunist who had sold his ideals—if he'd ever truly had any—for his name on a yacht. And he'd sold Rafe down the river, as well.

Terra's tense anticipation began to diffuse as Noel-Cooke began his concluding remarks. He wound up his speech and everyone applauded, and as Noel-Cooke stepped back from the podium, one of the banquet waiters hurried up to him with an envelope on a gleaming, silver, message tray.

The waiter, a mustachioed, carrot-top redhead in horn-rim glasses waited at attention while Noel-Cooke opened the envelope and read the message. Almost instantly, the diplomat stepped up to the podium again and cleared his throat several times.

"A few more words, ladies and gentlemen." The lights for the TV cameras picked up a sheen of sweat on Noel-Cooke's suntanned face. He took a handkerchief out and mopped his forehead, his cheeks, the back of his neck. "Words regarding . . ." He paused and reexamined the message as if it would explode any moment.

A murmur swept through the room at the visible change that had come over him. Sweat dripping off his chin, in fact.

"An estimable gentleman we all have heard much of in past years." He mopped again. "An unfairly maligned man, in fact, whose good name has been decimated for a crime he did not—I personally witness to you he did not—commit. He is Mr. Rafe Jermain and—"

The cameras zoomed in and the audience erupted, cutting him off. Elizabeth gripped the judge's arm.

"Of course Rafe was not a criminal," she maintained in a stout, steely voice. "Too little too late from this twit, whoever he thinks he is."

Lalie broke out in a broad smile and clasped Terra's hand. "Amen and a*men*."

Mr. Noel-Cooke, handkerchief soaked, had to shout to be heard, and what he continued to say tallied exactly with what Terra had heard from Rafe, except for any mention of Leon.

She bolted to her feet and scanned the room around and around, knowing Rafe had to be there somewhere. Where? Too many people were milling around to tell. Newspaper reporters were galloping out of the hall to phone home.

"Cameron," Elizabeth said, "where is Mr. Graves?"

The judge stood. "Somewhere near, I'm sure. I'll find him."

"I'll go with you," she said, and they left the table.

A chaos of sound ricocheted in the room, everyone talking at once, and Noel-Cooke shouting above it all that Rafe Jermain was *not* a traitor, repeat *not* a turncoat.

Terra stayed on her feet, scanning, searching the sea of faces. She saw Thomas Graves approaching the podium with Cameron. Graves tapped Noel-Cooke on the shoulder and the diplomat turned. They had a brief, animated discussion away from the microphone and Terra saw Graves examine the message. His eyebrows rose, and he stared hard for a moment at the waiter who'd delivered the silver tray.

Graves stepped to the podium, radiating a subtle power of command that quieted the audience and riveted all eyes on him. "The keynote addresses are postponed until further notice," he said. "Television coverage will also cease at this time. Please be seated so that coffee can be served. Thank you very much for your kind cooperation."

Simple words, powerfully spoken, they subdued the atmosphere and within moments the banquet had resumed a reasonable measure of its earlier pace.

Graves, Elizabeth and the judge left with Noel-Cooke and the waiter in tow. The chatter in the room lowered accordingly.

Terra sat down and said to Lalie. "Do you see Rafe anywhere?"

"Nowhere. But I have a feeling it won't be long. Speaking of feelings, Terra..." She gave a double thumbs-up.

"Lalie, thank heaven he's alive. I'm dying to see him."

"I know," Lalie replied, "and I'm dying to see the wedding you two are going to have."

Terra shook her head wistfully. "Rafe was set against it when I left. In fact, I don't know why I'm sitting here feeling so relieved and happy, except because it seems he's alive. It's not as if I have a future with him."

Suddenly a hand came from behind her and settled on her shoulder. She gasped, tipped her head back and looked up at the banquet waiter who'd delivered the message to Noel-Cooke. The mustachioed, carrot-top waiter in horn rims. Up close she saw that his eyes were deep blue behind the thick, lightly tinted lenses.

"Don't say a word," he commanded before either she or Lalie could exclaim with surprise. "Come with me."

They followed him out of the banquet hall to Thomas Graves's office. Elizabeth and Cameron were there on the office couch, hugging, crying happy tears. Graves, in his desk chair, was blinking moisture from his own eyes.

Rafe shut the door, took off the glasses and stripped off his fake mustache. He gave Lalie a big hug, then took Terra in his arms and kissed her long and sweet.

He turned with her to his grandparents and announced, "Meet my future wife." Then he immediately turned back to her and asked, "What are you doing here?"

"She had a feeling," Lalie supplied. "A Leon feeling about Noel-Cooke."

Rafe raised his eyebrows. "Well, is my future wife brilliant or what?"

Terra didn't know what to say about being Rafe's future wife, so she asked, "Where is Leon?"

"Having a word with a federal agent in another office," Graves said.

Then she asked Rafe, "How did you slip through security here?"

"Stole a banquet waiter's union card ID at that hotel in Charleston." He touched his red hair and eyebrows. "Had a couple of Clairol moments."

"How did you make Noel-Cooke talk?"

"Gave him a note that said his wife, children and yacht were in the gravest possible danger if he didn't. Gave him a look at my eyes, too, when I served him the note. I think the yacht did the trick, though."

"Rafe," said Elizabeth, dabbing at her eyes, "you always were the nicest possible bad boy. You've proven it once again to one and all."

Cameron gave him a power sign. "Good to have you back with us."

Rafe nodded. "In jail probably for a while, if not longer."

Elizabeth shook her head. "Oh, no. I'll put up the resort for bail if that becomes necessary. The entire property." She smiled at Terra. "How did you and Rafe coalesce in the midst of everything?"

"Someday when we both have time, Miz Elizabeth, I'll tell you the whole incredible story."

"Long one," Rafe confirmed. "Two whole weeks."

Graves stood from his desk. "I don't know about the rest of you, but I've got an overcrowded banquet hall to keep an eye on."

"And so do we," Elizabeth said, rising along with Cameron.

They all left the office, followed by Lalie who wondered aloud where in heaven Liz was whenever there was a crisis. The answer to that, it seemed, might never be known.

Alone together, Terra and Rafe embraced. He rested his forehead against hers. "I've had a change of heart since you last saw me, Terra. A week without you did it."

"What do you mean?"

"I need to settle down. With you and Josh, if you'll both have me."

She gave him a kiss that told him she'd have him without any doubt. "We've got some rough waters ahead, I know," she said, "but in the end we'll have what we want and need."

"Say you'll marry me, Terra."

"I will," she promised. "But first, there's something you need to know."

He groaned. "Don't tell me you've got to get a divorce or annulment first. God, just when I think I'm going to get the wife and stepson of my biggest dreams, there's something I don't know?"

"Mmm-hmm. You're getting a wife and *son*."

"Come again?"

"Sit down, Rafe." She led him to the couch. "You once said I reminded you of someone you knew. Mermaid?"

He gave her a quizzical look. "So?"

"Rafe, can you picture me five years younger, fifteen pounds slimmer, with long, blond hair?"

Rafe frowned, then his eyes widened. "How do you . . . Wait a minute, I never said she was . . ."

"I was blond, once, Rafe. Five years ago, the night before you put out to sea from Charleston Harbor."

He drew back, looking thunderstruck. "You mean, you're my Mermaid?"

"One and the same."

Rafe stared at her, not saying anything for so long that she started to think he'd gone into shock. She touched his hand and he came to life, recognition dawning in his eyes.

"Terra, you've got me speechless." He swallowed hard, obviously searching for words. "But now I see it."

She drew a deep breath. "Rafe, Josh is our son."

There was another startled silence, and then his blue eyes misted. "Well, glory be," he murmured. "Josh Jermain."

Terra nodded. "We're a family, if you want one."

Closing his eyes, Rafe gathered her in his arms and held her as her words sank in. Pillowed against his chest, Terra sighed.

Everything, finally, was going to be all right.

Epilogue

A YEAR LATER, on a lovely day in May, Terra and Rafe were married at Bride's Bay Resort. Surrounded by dearly beloved family and friends, they made their vows to Judge Bradshaw in the rose garden gazebo.

The best man, Kent Prescott, and Macy Medford, the maid of honor, were the happiest friends at the event. People were already predicting they'd be the next newlyweds at Bride's Bay. Of course, Macy caught the bouquet.

All charges against Rafe had been dropped, and with his name in the clear at last he'd made a full recovery. In fact, Terra thought he'd never looked better. He was breathtakingly handsome in his charcoal gray tux. He wore a pink rosebud in his lapel.

As for Rafe, he thought he'd never seen anything so beautiful as Terra, his wife, mother of his son, standing at his side. She looked like a mermaid princess in pearls and white satin, her veil flowing around her bare shoulders.

But perhaps the happiest family member witnessing their marriage was Joshua Andrew Jermain, who'd always wanted a father and got the real thing when his mommy married his daddy.

A PERFECT
FAMILY

But shocking revelations and heartache lie just
beneath the surface of their charmed lives

*Mills & Boon are proud to bring you this thrilling
family saga from international bestselling author,
Penny Jordan.*

Long-held resentments and jealousies are reawakened when three
generations of the Crighton family gather for a special birthday
celebration—revealing a family far from perfect underneath!

Available: September 1997   Price: £4.99 (384pp)

✳ 50p off A Perfect Family ✳

Spoil yourself next month
with these four novels from

THE HEARTBREAK KID by Alison Kent

Tyler Barnes had a healthy masculine ego, not to mention a
heartbreaking grin and an incredible body. But Sophie North was
only passing through and she'd sworn never to live her life at the
mercy of her own passionate nature. But Sophie should have
known, nature *always* gets its own way...

THE LAST MAN IN MONTANA by Kristine Rolofson

Bachelors & Booties

Will Cody returned to his ranch to sell his inheritance. Family
life, staying in any one place for too long just isn't for him—
until he meets the new 'foreman', Becky McGregor. She's
gorgeous, sexy and a *mother*! She's determined he should keep
the ranch...

THE ALL-AMERICAN MALE by Glenda Sanders

Cassaundra Snow was thrilled when she met Chuck Granger, but
as powerful as her response to him was, she dreaded the moment
when his reporter's instincts would tell him that she was living
out a fairy tale. And that her story was Cinderella *in reverse*...

SEX, LIES AND LEPRECHAUNS by Renee Roszel

Devlin Rafferty was as handsome as the devil, but Laura Todd
was a woman with a mission—to find the heir to a fortune—so
she couldn't afford to be distracted while she was in Ireland. But
maybe a pleasurable little diversion would be all right. Except it
became more than a diversion and it was a bit *too* pleasurable...

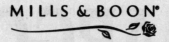

MILLS & BOON®

Back by Popular Demand

Available from September 1997

A collector's edition of favourite titles from one of
Mills & Boon's best-loved romance authors.

Don't miss this wonderful collection of sought-after
titles, now reissued in beautifully matching volumes
and presented as one cherished collection.

Look out next month for:

Title #1	**Jake Howard's Wife**
Title #2	**Scorpions' Dance**

Free Book offer!
see books 1 & 2 for details

Available wherever Mills & Boon books are sold

MARGOT DALTON

first Impression

Be *very* careful who you trust.

A child is missing and the only witness tells a chilling
story of what he's 'seen'. Jackie Kaminsky has three
choices. Dismiss the man as a handsome nutcase. Arrest
him as the only suspect. Or believe him.

"Detective Jackie Kaminsky leads a cast of fine-
ly drawn characters... An engrossing read."
—Publishers Weekly

"Jackie Kaminsky is a great addition to the
growing list of fictional detectives."
—Romantic Times

**AVAILABLE IN PAPERBACK
FROM AUGUST 1997**

EMMA DARCY

*at her most daring with an
unforgettable tale of ruthless sacrifice
and single-minded seduction*

THE SECRETS WITHIN

When Tamara Vandlier learns that her mother is dying
she is elated—and returns to the family estate to
destroy her mother's few remaining months, in
return for her own ruined childhood. Loyalty turns
to open rivalry in this novel that explores the dark,
hidden secrets of two branches of a powerful
Australian family.

**AVAILABLE IN PAPERBACK
FROM AUGUST 1997**

Bureau de Change

How would you like to win a year's supply of Mills & Boon® books? Well you can and they're FREE! Simply complete the competition below and send it to us by 28th February 1998. The first five correct entries picked after the closing date will each win a year's subscription to the Mills & Boon series of their choice. What could be easier?

1.	Lira	Sweden	____
2.	Franc	U.S.A.	____
3.	Krona	Sth. Africa	____
4.	Escudo	Spain	____
5.	Deutschmark	Austria	____
6.	Schilling	Greece	____
7.	Drachma	Japan	____
8.	Dollar	India	____
9.	Rand	Portugal	_4_
10.	Peseta	Germany	____
11.	Yen	France	____
12.	Rupee	Italy	____

C7H

Please turn over for details of how to enter...

How to enter...

It's that time of year again when most people like to pack their suitcases and head off on holiday to relax. That usually means a visit to the Bureau de Change... Overleaf there are twelve foreign countries and twelve currencies which belong to them but unfortunately they're all in a muddle! All you have to do is match each currency to its country by putting the number of the currency on the line beside the correct country. One of them is done for you! Don't forget to fill in your name and address in the space provided below and pop this page in a envelope (you don't even need a stamp) and post it today. Hurry competition ends 28th February 1998.

Mills & Boon Bureau de Change Competition
FREEPOST, Croydon, Surrey, CR9 3WZ
EIRE readers send competition to PO Box 4546, Dublin 24.

Please tick the series you would like to receive if you are a winner
Presents™ ❏   Enchanted™ ❏   Temptation® ❏
Medical Romance™ ❏   Historical Romance™ ❏

Are you a Reader Service™ Subscriber?   Yes ❏   No ❏

Ms/Mrs/Miss/Mr_____
(BLOCK CAPS PLEASE)

Address_____

_____

_____ Postcode_____

(I am over 18 years of age)